The People of Moorluke

Also by Georg Engel from K A Nitz:

Thy Neighbour's Wife

The Famine Village and Other Tales

Sorceress Circe: A Berlin Romance

The Burden

The Fear Before the Wife

Tales of the Forbidden

The Rider on the Rainbow

The People of Moorluke

Georg Engel

K A Nitz
ALBANY, NEW ZEALAND

Contents

CANTANKEROUS DURTIG

"No, old girl", wailed Hinrich Bull, the only one in the coastal village of Trent to deserve the name of a big fisherman, and at the same time, he struck together ringing the tall gleaming boots, which a former military bather had left behind by mistake, but which were now used by Hinrich as a badge of his extraordinary and outstanding worth.

"No, old girl," he complained and grasped chagrined at his plump bulbous nose which peered out ripe and bluish between his thick cheeks like a beautiful potato between the topsoil at harvest time. "No, old girl, what's going on with our daughter Durtig, dear God only knows. Look, if she had taken after me or you then she would have had to have had from me the great, masculine, considered insight into all business, and also a great power of resistance and patience towards that which can bring up human malice. For you must admit it, Minnie, that at the times when you get your weekly vehemence, I am always deaf in the right ear and blind in the left eye. Will you concede me that? Yes, you concede me that. And look, I want to tell you something good too. She would have had to have had purely from you the great friendliness and feminine loveliness in her face. I mean, from the beginning. For in retrospect, Minnie — don't take it wrong — you have some of that tendency to slander and gossip. Well, yes, that is just women's pleasure. And what now has our daughter Durtig inherited from the both of us? Not a thing. Not the understanding of money business from me, for look, think, is such a thing humanly possible? There she has last week let herself be talked by the old scissor grinder Rütebusch into buying a songbird. For a mark. For an entire mark. I thought I would fall down when I got to hear that. A mark for a bird which must still eat so much food. That is not my daughter at all. And has she perhaps received ample loveliness from you? I mean at least in the face? Not a trace. If a young man aims a word at her, then he must be afraid that she does not immediately scratch out his eyes. And if a woman ever wants to kiss and be fond with her, then she must protect herself from a beating. When someone says 'hello' or 'nice day' to her, she spits on their boots. And when she recently stood as a godparent together with the harbourmaster's son before the holy altar, she gave him a ringing slap right in front of the Pastor. And why? Because the boy thought she had such pretty white skin. Now I ask you, old girl, because you possess a pretty white skin, must she thus administer the harbourmaster's son, who has 10,000 marks of his own — 10,000, Minnie — a slap? What shall become of the girl now? I ask you that as a poor defeated man. For in other houses, such a girl who bites off a neck and nose is already long since gone and out of the business. But do you perhaps know someone who would dare that with her and take her up? — I don't. For look, although I am her own father, I would rather sit for ten cold nights on the roof than with our Durtig so prettily cosy and bride-like in a secluded room. But what shall be done now? I ask you."

Then the tall, heavy-boned fisherwoman slapped the colourful woolen shirt with a mighty blow onto the edge of the wash tub full of strong-smelling foaming soap, wiped her mouth with her bare arm as she prepared to speak, and then directed her sparkling blue eyes large and menacingly to her husband who was looking down serenely at his gleaming boots.

"You're to blame for that, Hinrich", she responded roughly.

"What? Me, Minnie?"

"Yes, you, Hinrich", it sounded unchanged, hard and accusatory. "If you had passed on all your plain attributes now — I don't want to speak about it, for I never complain — I mean, then you would have to give such a worm something enticing to go on its way."

The husband nodded heavily, "Well, then do that, wife", he agreed approvingly. "Why do you not give her anything enticing then? A red dress or a white petticoat or ..."

"That's bells and whistles", the mother cut him off reluctantly. "You have to give a royal trousseau to such a misfortune of a woman. That is the enticing. I tell you. Hinrich ..."

"No, wife ...", the leading fisherman sprang up and slapped his trouser pockets, "that I won't do, and that I can't do. For I don't have as much money as it needs to cover up our loving and cantankerous daughter, wife. For we would end up simply begging, and you could then go through the countryside with your bag of gossip. But look, Minnie, fortune wants to do us well. What do you say, out there before our kitchen window I see right now the lame scissor grinder Rütebusch. And what he tells us, we will do, for he goes far over the countryside, and is well equipped for such antics. Take him coffee, but don't offer it to him straightaway. He has certainly also already drunk."

And see, directly as the worried parents were thus speaking, the fresh hum of the grinding wheel rang out from outside, and at the same time, a strange, squeaky voice sang the old rhyming phrase:

> Hurry, hurry, hurry,
> Scurry, scurry, scurry,
> Grinder turning fresh and plain,
> Make the knife sharp again,
> Whet the tool and the shear,
> Thus, people, bring me here
> All that rusts in the house,
> Cause it helps and costs nout.
> Come to the wheel, hurry, hurry,
> Bring the knives, scurry, scurry.

The fisherman's wife opened the window and called out something. You could not claim that it would have sounded especially inviting, "Stop, Stöffe Rütebusch, you may come in."

But the eccentric figure of the scissor grinder bowed deeply at first, and as he swept back delicately with his club foot, he performed with his right hand, which was missing its little finger, a widely discharging gesture of greeting. No royal marshal could have performed it more solemnly, "Beautiful, delightful, happy good morning, proud young lady", he squeaked, and at the same time opened his toothless mouth crookedly with it strangely grey stubbled surround. "One becomes ever more beautiful, Mrs Bull. One rounds out in the loving breast and becomes more slender around the pleasing hips. It is magnificent! It becomes an ever cosier femininity. Have you perhaps otherwise rusty knives or blunt scissors? My craftsmanship has risen significantly in the month particularly. In fact since I had the honour of being permitted to sharpen the collected kitchen knives and ornate cutlery of the Tsar of Russia on this here subservient wheel. Hurry, hurry, hurry. In what way can I be of assistance, delightful young lady?"

"You are a muttonhead, Stöffe", the stately fisherman threw in-between very definitely, having appeared at the front door. "Do you want to wait first until she has shut the window and booted you in here herself? You know Minnie keeps up the regiment."

"To serve — to serve —", Stöffe whimpered reverentially in-between, whereby he again performed a deep bow in the direction of the window, "She is a sovereign. Emperor and Pope in one person. Where will I allow myself to have even just one objection to such high wishes? I am coming, Hinrich, I am right in her charming vicinity, venerable reigning lady. Whoops!"

With that he gave his strangely eccentric body a swing, and hobbled amidst everlasting greetings over to the leading fisherman, until he, wheezing and snorting from the effort, stood in the wide brownish, fisherman's room.

The fisherman's wife made a gesture. You could have assumed that she was commanding the guest to sit down on the black leather sofa. And before the scissor grinder had found time to make his delight known over the glorious residence through his well-known exclamations, "A castle — a paradise — a veritable, ladies' cabin", for he considered this last to be the finest of all, Hinrich Bull had already pressed him down roughly on the shiny leather, and his wife began, like all great characters, in the middle of her train of thought, "Yes, just that, because of the final marriage of Durtig."

The scissor grinder placed his left hand on his heart, and with his four-fingered right hand, he began blowing kisses in the air, "A rare young lady", he stammered, enraptured. "A select exemplar of feminine glamour. I have fallen head over heels in love. I know all the princes, and all the leading fishermen's sons from the district are already arriving at the house, proud Mrs Bull."

Then the mother stamped hard with her foot. The glasses and vases on the windowsills and cupboards trembled and swayed as a result, "Rubbish," she burst out darkly, "we don't know in from out anymore. Are you familiar, Stöffe, with how Durtig recently behaved with the harbourmaster's son?"

"Yes — yes — talk of the day — everywhere of nothing else. Played a bit of pancake flipping with him. Why not? A charming child's play."

And now both parents began confusedly reciting their complaints and fears about the future.

"What does one do?" Mrs Bull wailed in conclusion, as she wrung her bony hands, and her husband scratched behind his ear, murmuring, "Who will take on such a monster?"

Stöffe Rütebusch sat for a while quite still on his leather sofa, right under the massive strawflower wreath, and by the twitching of the skewed corners of his mouth, and by the blinking of his crafty brown eyes, you could note that all sorts of roguish tricks were whirling through his head. But then he suddenly started, and as he pressed the fisherwoman's blue skirt at its outermost edge emphatically to his lips, he stuttered with enthusiasm, "An inspiration, ladies and gentlemen, an idea from the higher religions. Listen to me. Your gracious daughter has gotten a bit — how do I express this? — a bit lively. What is that? Liveliness is a high virtue. But it requires a quite special and insightful treatment. There I once saw at the horse market in Grimmen a piece played by a precious and noble society of comedians. Such a foxy and mad wench was also there — pardon me, Mrs Bull, I mean only the theatrical woman at the time by that — and she too could not be brought under the bonnet for a long time. Look, and what had the comedians at the horse market in Grimmen devised? They acquired for the lively young lady an even more lively and friskier man. Ha, Mrs Bull, but that would make you a ticklish and delightful event. If she hurled a pot, then the vagabond suggested that it wasn't yet enough, and threw all the kitchen equipment after it. They smashed the potter Holzkopf's entire stand of crockery. The young, delicate woman then passed her hand with all ten fingers through his hair, then the newly wed cried that was not proper kissing. And then he embraced her lovingly and squeezed her to him so that her bones made proper music. And when she then tried to scream and rage, he laughed that he could sing even better. And with that he began to roar and lament so that the frisky woman fell into a genuine faint. Look, Madame Bull and leading fisherman Hinrich, you must provide such a bridegroom and indulgent surrendering of the heart for your temperamental daughter Miss Durtig. And if you hand me thus ten genuine Prussian talers ... easy — easy, gentlefolk, I mean just for the necessary outlays — — — if you want to grant me this tiny bridal sum, then I would deliver you this evening the happy and expectant son-in-law. He will make no claims, Mr Hinrich. He is, as I know him, merely doing it for the honour and the distinguished family. And now think on that. And when I have sharpened my knives outside, then tell me your decisive answer. Beautiful, young lady, I kiss your skirt hem — Mr Hinrich, I remain as always —."

A minute later, Stöffe Rütebusch stood again before his cart and squeaked with his high falsetto voice to the rolling and whirring of his wheel, while red-twitching sparks sprayed forth in sheaves under his fingers:

> Hurry, hurry, hurry,
> Scurry, scurry, scurry — —

***

It is about the hour of dusk. The sea sleeps already and rests under a cosy grey blanket of mist. A dreary moon watches over this great rest like a dim night light which a solicitous hand has placed at a secure distance.

But in the wealthy fisherman's house of Hinrich Bull, it is becoming more festive. A large lamp of black porcelain is burning there on the white-covered table, and just now Mrs Bull is carrying a sort of serving dish in on a large wooden board. There is also eel and steaming potatoes.

That is a main course and very fine.

And so strange does this unusual array appear, that Durtig-Sophie, who is ordering her exquisite red spray of hair before the mirror of the cleaning cabinet, throws an astonished look from her dark eyes at her excited mother.

The look has a sharp and drilling effect.

"What's going on today?", the twenty year old asked with such a soft, clear sounding voice that you could not conceive at all that this red, softly curved mouth could spray such an abundance of spite and cursing in angry hours. "What's happening?"

The leading fisherman's wife barely moves her head, but she nevertheless clears her throat a little self-consciously, before she quickly bursts out her answer, "There are visitors!"

The redhead throws back vigorously the spraying flickers, "Not for me", issues from her curtly.

"What?"

"I'm going to bed."

However, her mother does not answer this threat, but strides immediately to act to settle it. With a vigorous movement namely, she has reached the door, so as to lock it with an audible rattle of the key, "So, my daughter," she utters now satisfied, "now go."

"But I don't want to — don't want to —", the gently curving mouth of Durtig-Sophie suddenly shrieks in remarkable, somersaulting notes which strike quite strangely against her previously mild talk, and at the same time, her little foot stamps pithily on the floorboards. "If I don't want to, then I just will not. What's going on then? What are you planning again? Who is coming today?"

"Eh, Durtig, someone quite superfine."

"So? I can imagine. But that I won't say, mother," and at the same time, she threw her outstretched hand diagonally through the air, "that ass can congratulate himself, for look, I will smack him straightaway over the back of the head."

"Wait," her mother cried, and the blood rose hotly in her head with worry over the threatening collapse of her hopes for the future, "do you, girl, want the distinguished and noble house of your dear father — —."

Only, she got no further in her rebuke. For there was suddenly a beating on the locked door outside with both fists, and the anxious voice of Hinrich Bull penetrated, hoarse with agitation, "Open up — open up — for God's sake, quick, they are coming."

And when the leading fisherman had appeared in the gleam of his tall topboots breathlessly before both the women, he still had time to raise both hands up in confusion, stammering, "Minnie, you will be amazed, such a thing I have never seen before."

Then fate was pounding at the door. It went quite still in the room. And then, no, truly, a procession followed as had neither been seen, nor even held for possible in the fishing village of Trent ever before. In a long and creased frock coat which the scissor grinder must have undoubtedly just hired from a rag shop, Stöffe Rütebusch hobbled in with his most exquisite bowing, which was so endless that the solemn dress split in the middle and showed his yellow woolen, brown stained work trousers, which cascaded down artlessly onto a pair of massive wooden clogs. With his four-fingered right hand, the guest pressed a fabulous top hat to his body, a monstrosity which could have just as well also swum in the sea as a signal buoy for straying ships, "Beautiful, entranced, well-fed, good evening, dignified family", he called delightedly, whereby he performed all sorts of delicate figures with his club foot. "We could not have resisted the revered invitation with honour and gladness, and here, Mrs Minnie and Mr Hinrich Bull, as well as treasured daughter Miss Durtig, here, look closely at him ..." — at these words, Stöffe swung his top hat in the direction of the door and completely assumed the countenance of a show booth operator who wishes to introduce a lion with an ape's head to a distinguished audience — "here we have Theder Wasmund, a man and a gentleman, as he appears not for the second time between the bay and the back country. And if you seek money from him, gentlefolk, there is nothing doing. Only fresh moved here through Stöffe Rütebusch, court scissor grinder to the Tsar of Russia and remunerated war invalid from the year '64 with visible wound. As said, that is Theder Wasmund."

And it was in fact worth watching the arrival attentively. The three Bulls stared quite speechlessly at him with necks stretched forward.

God preserve me, is it possible, it twitched discouragingly through the father Hinrich's brain. The beast will surely thrust his head through the ceiling.

"And what a forest of hair the creature has", Minnie was horrified, dropping her valiant hands in shock. "Lord Jesus and all the saints, from behind to below the bundled shirt front. It must surely be some sort of Samson from the Bible. My God, where did Rütebusch surely scare that up from? But he is steady. Durtig cannot confront that. Good grief, the feet," she added, breaking off.

And Durtig?

Dear God, during the reign of this long silence, she constantly watched the hands and arms of Theder Wasmund. They were a pair of oars which ended in two enormous paddles. It did not seem at all so impossible that the guest could sit the girl gently in his palms to then offer her to some admirer out the window.

Thus they looked at each other for a while. And it remained oddly that the giant also squinted with a pair of good-natured blue child-like eyes at the red-haired girl like a massive dog which has been excited by its master into leaping up, and now feels awe and timidity before the magnificence of a human body.

"Yes", Theder Wasmund murmured, and scratched behind his ear. Incidentally, he wore a black, second-hand frock coat just like his master, only both arms as well as the back-seam had already burst from his massive size, and down below, blue sailor's pants, and a pair of man-high gumboots peered forth.

They sat down at the table.

And during the excellent meal, the scissor grinder endeavoured to explain his show booth act more clearly, and make it more acceptable, "Yes, this thus, proud Mrs Bull, is Theder Wasmund. You will probably ask, beautiful young lady, where he is from. For every man born must accordingly have had a cradle and also befitting parents. But you merely think that is so. It is not at all necessary. Right, Theder?"

"Yes", the chewing giant murmured something in a low voice. His childlike nature, with these explanations, the more so as they were under the dark mocking eyes of Durtig-Sophie, who perpetually pursed her lips contemptuously, did not feel well at all, and his large blue boyish eyes steered constantly as if magnetically drawn to her cold, unapproachable features. He almost forgot the eel because of it. And it was a main course. "So, as I said, people, without parents and without cradle, that is the finest of all. For look, here lies the mysteriousness in fact, and someone could be a prince. Look at Theder, and then give me your considered answer. And then nothing more. He is a fisherman. But you surely do not believe that my friend Theder fishes like other people or their children? Pst, obey, dog, you are running on the wrong path. Excuse me, Mrs Bull, I do not mean you by that — but nets? Does not touch them. Theder fishes with his hands. Have you all ever seen such, considerate and patronising family? You may buy them from him. Right, Theder?"

And again the man bowed his head soundlessly and timidly. He had imagined this first appearance in the rich leading fisherman's family would be considerably lighter and cosier. And in his dull and unalert mind, an ever stronger urge to flight was stirring. No, this girl — she was surely a princess — and wondrously beautiful ... he had not thought about the like at all. And now he should simply take her away, she who smiled so mockingly and haughtily? And what darkly flashing beams shot from her eyes. Over on the island, he had once found in the forest a nest of young black snakes. They had also flashed and wreathed so similarly at the time, just like in these eyes. No, no, it was not so simple. He would like most of all to leave. But then what Stöffe Rütebusch had told him arose before his raw disposition anew in gleaming colours. The wealth, the enormous wealth. And to not have to serve anymore. And even being a gentleman, a leading fisherman perhaps, no, no, he should stay and wait a little yet. And again he looked down at his plate, and felt, as it passed behind him over his steer's neck uncomfortably, how the girl's gaze glided away from him hostilely.

***

Then came the hour which would become the wildest and most incomprehensible in Durtig's existence.

Days — weeks later, when she crouched with her red glimmering head, behind the beach boulders at the bay, like an enormous piece of amber washed up from antiquity, then, at the thought of this one hour, her limbs were laced together by an aching spasm, and all her strength escaped her suddenly worn-out joints.

Ugh, ugh, it was all not real — an awful, vicious dream. Oh, she would strike out, with both fists, to shoo away this nasty spectre. But then, then this strange languor again nestled in her usually so eel-like supple body, and with a dull murmur and wide-open, horrified eyes which buried themselves in the infinity away across the sea, she collapsed anew.

Just wait, wait — ugh, ugh — oh, she would avenge herself.

How did it happen though? ... Yes, yes, it had happened so.

Quite unexpectedly — no, no, it certainly all happened by secret agreement, that rogue Rütebusch had certainly arranged it all so — there she was after that first festive dinner suddenly left alone with the uncouth giant in the large brown, best room of the Bulls'.

"No, no," she had cried out furiously at the time, "we have not wagered thus", and with her shaking hands, she rattled the locked door. "Oh, this roguery", for she could hear quite distinctly outside how her parents were lingering with the scissor grinder in the hallway to listen from there for the result of this strangest courtship of all.

In doubled rage, she then struck against the wood. More and more powerfully and furiously until it rang out dully over the dark village street and across the empty expanse of the sea.

"Open up — let me out — I will wreck this place if you do not unlock it."

Only everything remained still, and she only heard the shrill voice of the scissor grinder giggle, "Hinrich, now it has come. Now Theder Wasmund gets to work. Gentlefolk, it is a blue and green wonder."

Then the girl leapt back. She suddenly rose up quite close before the Hun-like figure who seemed to have followed the entire incident up to then motionlessly and with unmeasured astonishment. Yes, an amused smile played around the mouth of the giant, a mouth shaded by a boyish, blond down.

In his sluggish, unspoilt mood, he contemplated what should happen now, surely first of all a magnificent joke, a prank over which the now so furious, red-headed creature here, once everything was over, would certainly laugh over heartily with him. Absolutely — had everything not been promised and confirmed to him? Had not the esteemed fisherfolk winked constantly at him in secret? What then did the redhead want? For it remained clear that there was no opposition on this earth on the part of her parents.

Well, then you begin, Theder Wasmund thought, eager for action. The little one would surely gradually recognise his rationale.

He slowly approached her and ponderously stretched out to her his paw, which was so monstrous that Durtig-Sophie was beset anew by a shudder before this living shovel alone. Quite without wanting, the tears began shooting suddenly from her dark eyes. But the giant did not notice that they were tears of fury.

He began, "Miss, I want to make it short, for everything is agreed upon, and the thing can well please me. And I liked the the beautiful beer, and the beautiful eel too. And, Miss, you yourself — if I also have no prac-

tice in it, for I have never had a bride, but so far as I understand that you …".

"What? What?" Durtig-Sophie screamed, possessing
the feeling all the time that the storm were howling
about her ears and she must undoubtedly drown, "what
is that about me?"

"You, Miss," the shocked man stuttered onward, "you
are such a pretty, red gingerbread on the Christmas
tree. Or like such a young, four week old pony which
you would like to stroke over the back with your hand.
And the red hair —", he rubbed his head, searching,
"such looks well like a small box of gold coins, quite
new, which I have never seen gathered together before.
But, glorious Miss, what's that?"

Then Durtig was at him. She wanted directly to
punch with her fist the lips which had brought forth so
much mockery, as she believed. Only, even if she had
sprung up, she would not have reached the towering
man. Then her burning, boiling-over fury passed into
something still more discreditable. Hey, that was good.
It extinguished her wildly flickering fire as if a breaker
had swept her away.

She stretched up on tiptoe, and as she grasped and
shook the blue sailor's vest of her enemy with both
hands, she spat contemptuously and desperately right
in his face.

Then she herself emitted a scream as if she had been
struck.

But what was that? When she again dared to look up,
her opposite still stood unchanged, and did not stir.
Without having shifted, the giant figure remained, and
only the massive hands were clasped as if they had sympathy with someone deserving of mercy, or as if they
wanted to keep him from a great, outrageous sin. The
lumbering head moved back and forth at the same time
uncomprehendingly, and genuine sadness had appeared

in the boyish blue eyes. "Miss," he said finally, quite calmly, and just with great, honest amazement, "what did you do then? I cannot have done anything for it? For it should all be so. And look, I meant it also right, right well with you. But you will surely see it yourself now, what is promised is promised. Now I cannot go back anymore, else I must shame myself before Stöffe Rütebusch, and before the eyes of your own parents. And about that which you have done to me, we will both preserve silence over. Though I will never ever forget it surely. But we know it now, and the others, they need not learn of it. Right?"

As he spoke this ingenuously like a little defeated boy, he stretched his shovel-hand out to her once more for confirmation as it were. But the fury now resided once more in Durtig-Sophie. It prevented her from being able to see, to gaze at the lowered, sad, boyish eyes, nor even hear the honest, reproachfully booming voice. No, she rather sprang anew, and heaved with all her might her little fist into the proffered giant fingers.

"Oh, you rogue, you burglar", she cried almost senselessly, and yet in full triumph, because she had remained superior to this enormous man-child up to now. "I want to clean you out. Do you know that? I will sweep you out with our common kitchen broom. And then onto the rubbish heap, for there you belong. Such a fellow from whom you can buy all sorts of infamous deeds with money? Ugh, are you not ashamed? You big beanpole? But wait, now I will give you my answer straightaway."

With that she went like someone possessed into the corner, and actually reached for the broom.

Only she was not permitted to do that. This threat spoke quite distinctly to the understanding of the unfortunate suitor. Here the being of the redhead, till then so strange, again made concessions to the giant's trust and familiarity. It shot gloomily red over the so patient boyish countenance. With one of his enormous strides, he was next to her.

"Leave it!", he demanded firmly and menacing.

And when she nevertheless, as if despairing, clasped the wooden handle, then what Durtig-Sophie could never ever forget happened, what she trembled over when she was lying lost by the beach boulders.

With a laugh which suddenly burst out, never heard before and blaring over everything, the giant abruptly raised the floundering girl in his arms, which closed under and over her like a pair of freshly hewn roof beams.

"Help, help", Durtig-Sophie cried, as she already felt how her mind was sinking into a blue hazy abyss. And as it were from a great distance, she heard yet how the blaring voice called into her ear, "No, no, girl, have no fear. I am just making you quiet. For you must not scream anymore if we shall continue to tolerate each other. And of beating, look, there can be no more talk of that between us either; because Pastor Witt will not marry such couples. And you are my bride now, and will remain so too. Now right. For I need you, and what you bring with you, far too needfully. Else I would surely still reconsider it."

And with that he placed his hand on her mouth as he carried his burden like a child's toy to the door which had immediately opened before him.

Towering and triumphant, he stood there on the floor where the leading fisherman's family surrounded him in rigid astonishment. The scissor grinder, however, sprang over to Mrs Bull, grasped again her blue skirt at its outer hem, and as he pressed it to his lips with his accustomed solemnity, he crowed in extreme delight, "What did I say, highly delighted young mother? Theder Wasmund is the greatest. He is in a realm like you have never seen before. And when you think you know him, say cheers, for you have not known him for long. What did I say? Your daughter, Miss Durtig, is in a complete bridal silence. Does she feel it, look at the still white dove calm in Theder's arms. — She does not stir."

Thus he spoke.

But Durtig-Sophie was unconscious.

***

When Stöffe Rütebusch later told of the ensuing engagement, his club foot usually shook with laughter, he made the most beautiful red flashes spray from his wheel before his audience at the annual fair or at the great shooting festival, and crowed finally in the greatest delight, "Yes, see, children, esteemed patrons and devoted community, that was yet something. They both at first had nothing to do with the usual bride and bridegroom nodding. As soon as Durtig in fact, the sweet pious creature, saw him coming, she chucked a stone at him. Or poured a bucket of milk from the dormer window over him; that was such a little bridal teasing. Hurry, hurry, hurry! And when she then screamed at him, red with fury, 'You klutz, you miserable mast, you don't think perhaps that I will take you, you boar, you?' — then Theder Wasmund nodded at her amiably, the big, august, the honest Theder Wasmund, he blew her a kiss — and what a one, gentlefolk — and he suggested quite gently and simply, 'Yes, yes, I know it all, my sweetheart, you cannot endure it at all anymore. But fourteen days from now, then you will have me, my treasure. Until then you must keep patient.' For such phrases, I had made him study them with seriousness and science. And the devil knows where he got the knack. Even when the girl crept from him into the most accursed and darkest hiding holes, he always knew straightaway to track her down. Hurry, hurry, hurry! I think Theder managed it through sense of smell. He merely raised his nose a little in the air, and swoop, he had caught his little love. Patrons, you can believe me, once he even pulled her out from Minnie's oven. When it now came to the morning of the wedding — — — hurry, hurry, hurry, no, beautiful women and noble men, you will not doubt my proven trustworthiness? — look, there the devil set loose. For Durtig did not want it. She sat there in her greyest and shabbiest coat of all as she constantly worked about amongst the peat and coal so that she could smear her face nicely. But Theder, my truly correct and genuine Theder, he tapped her trustingly on the shoulder, and said, 'sweet, it is rightly so. Always without much fuss. And so that you don't dirty your little feet in the deep dirt path, I will carry you into the church. You know, my dear, how appetisingly I do that.' — Here though, gentlefolk, was where now the maddest and strangest thing of all happened. At his inviting word in fact, Durtig at once stood up stiff and rigid. She was so pale — how shall I say it? — well then like a porcelain mug full of milk. And then she spoke so to herself as she just squeezed together her little fists, and looked with her dark eyes at my Theder quite funnily, 'Good, then we will go. You want it that way. And my father and mother want it that way too. But later, then I will have my say. Now quick.' And with that she calmly gave him her hand, and let herself be led like a lamb to the church. Hurry, hurry, hurry. Noble patrons and delightful ladies, the only people at the wedding were Mr Hinrich and Mrs Minnie Bull as well as the the well-known scissor grinder to the Tsar of Russia, knives for five pfennigs. And they cried there as if grain were being shot into a water butt. And the only ones who kissed each other after the wedding were Hinrich and Minnie, and the aforesaid scissor grinder. Always in turn. But the bride and groom did not stir. So, well-meaning patrons. And if you should now miss the marriage sermon of Pastor Witt in particular, that will cost ten pfennigs more, with simultaneous grinding of blunt scissors. I remain, as always — — hurry, hurry, hurry! Scurry, scurry, scurry!"

***

But what the all-knowing Stöffe Rütebusch could not report on consisted entirely of a small inconsiderable circumstance.

Singing and whistling, the new husband had led his young better half to a tiny fisherman's cottage with a fishing boat belonging to it which had been meaningfully handed over to him by Hinrich as the only dowry. With the words, "Hard money, my boy. Lots, lots of money. With that though it is enough now too. Now do your thing."

And Theder Wasmund was quite convinced that he must succeed and be happy in every respect. Had the advice of Stöffe Rütebusch, the wise man of Trent, not preserved him from the worst? Truly, it was not to be believed. Now he, the have-nothing, possessed a house, a boat, and even a proper, young wife. Though the latter — the giant squinted inquiringly at the calmly striding girl on the way – behaved actually quite peculiarly. She had not yet directed the slightest word to him during the entire celebration, and when she now entered the house at the evening hour, Durtig-Sophie immediately strode to the stove to light a cheerful fire. Always in silence.

Eh what, the giant thought hopefully, and shook his big head convinced that when the moon came up, then she would surely be permitted to speak. It was probably all merely the fashion of women.

And whistling and singing, he stepped behind the busy woman to stroke her back shyly and timidly with his little giant's finger.

Then Durtig-Sophie shook herself as if a beetle were creeping over her skin, breathed deeply, and stepped to the side.

"What do you want?"

"Oh nothing at all, wifey."

"You should not say wifey to me."

"Oh, how then, wifey?"

"I am called Durtig."

"Yes, but I thought —".

"Now you know", the woman concluded coldly.

Theder Wasmund stepped onto the red floor, and let his nets run through his fingers. All new, with fresh pieces of cork and silk lashing. Fine, fine. And at the same time, he pondered. She is surely merely a little shy, it went through his ponderous mind. And it is surely quite good that way for an innocent girl. But later, Theder, later, when the moon has first come up, then the last prophesy of Stöffe Rütebusch will also be fulfilled.

He looked through the low window, which looked out on the bay, for the night stars.

See, over the dark expanse of water, the evening star already sparkles alone, in a blue shimmer, and far back over the the jagged black treetops of the grove by the beach, there a greenish golden light was swelling up as if something new and unfamiliar wanted to reveal itself there.

Yes, yes, now it will soon rise, the giant pondered, and grasped his heart with an awkward gesture. Why was it hammering there so violently? Why was it grasping for his throat as if an invisible fist were seeking him? "Lord," the solitary man murmured, "whether I now just go to her again? Look, I can see her through the crack in the door as she lights the lamp. Oh, that is cosy. And all that belongs to me. Why does she not call me at all though? Well, perhaps she is waiting for when the moon first stands over our roof."

And the big man lingered in the deep darkness alone before the window, and followed with pounding heart how the sparkling, golden disc rolled on its blue path nearer and nearer.

***

The moonlight swims brightly in the white loft room with the sloping ceiling, in which Durtig-Sophie now looms before the large rustic bed and slowly begins putting away her clothes.

She is quite alone. But she thinks that is quite right. A perverse, mocking smile plays distinctly about her small, twitching mouth, "He is surely afraid too", she murmurs in strange satisfaction to herself. "Beautiful, beautiful. Did not expect anything else from the rogue."

But what is that? Has she deceived herself? She raises an ear towards the nearby low door. Are massive steps not tapping up the creaking wooden stairs there?

The young wife presses her hand to her breast. Then she firmly grasps with trembling fingers her white shirt under her slender neck as if unintentionally, "Good", it pours out hoarsely from her. "It's better if it happens soon. The man can rejoice."

Tall and erect, all her limbs tense, she awaited her enemy. From her red hair which the moon has awakened to crackling life, glowing sparks of copper seem to spray. Her breath gets short and spasmodic.

Then the narrow door opens creaking. "Durtig."

Strange, the awkward man out there barely surmises what he has just stammered. With large, wide-open boyish eyes, he stares almost appalled at the looming white figure. Not for anything in the world would his innate timidity have dared now to cross the threshold without her command. No, with wide outstretched, swaying arms rather, he holds his body away from the doorposts, always murmuring clueless or numbly incoherent words to himself, "Durtig — I thought — when the moon comes up ... and yet Stöffe Rütebusch said ...".

"What did he say, you clumsy oaf?", it sounds razor-sharp from within.

"Durtig", he repeats once more, and at the same time, the man stretches out his hand trembling as if he wants to invoke or request something divine, something standing over him. "You don't have to be angry with me. I don't understand it. But I thought, because we are married though — and Stöffe Rütebusch advised me so firmly ...".

Shocked, with a gurgling sound, he breaks off. Then the answer comes to him which would be decisive for his entire life.

An ugly contemptuous laugh shrills towards him. And as the silver flood of the moon caressingly veils two beautiful, bare womanly arms in brilliance and shimmer, it brings it completely reasoned and ice-clear to the ears of the waiting man, "Nothing is between us, you rogue. Never ever in your entire life, have you heard that? And if they have sold me to you, then you knew beforehand what you were getting into. Not so? Did I deceive you in any way? And now go and sit yourself with Stöffe Rütebusch whom you have to thank for your great fortune. He will perhaps kiss and stroke you. But over this threshold you will not set a foot. Or God have mercy on you."

As the white figure had emitted these words amidst cutting scorn and stabbing contempt, as it were as if she had been preparing for it for months, she strode cold-bloodedly and erect to the door which she threw shut with a resounding blow. The noise echoed in the small, fisherman's cottage, then the same dull calm settled over everything anew.

But what drives the powerful, gigantic man who could with a kick of his enormous gumboot demolish this tiny partition wall of a wooden door? Why does he not strike out with his fist to obtain his rights with raw power? None of all that.

In this darkness, under the weaving black shadows of night, he crouches on the uppermost landing of the stairs. Soon he lays his head billowing with hair quite lightly and carefully at the door to listen fearfully and with restrained breath, and then he leads his giant finger to his mouth, shaking his head, bit on it so that the blood began to flow, and groaned gurgling to himself so that it sounded lost and broken, "Yes, but, how is that? — For want of the pure mercy of God, have I done something here? — Stöffe Rütebusch told me though ... And will it remain so forever? — God, God, something isn't right here ... who will help me out? — And — and what red hair she has, like a flame. — And the beautiful, beautiful arms. — I don't know at all whether I may think of them? — Lord in heaven, give me light in the darkness, for I cannot find a way out."

***

After a year and a day, Theder Wasmund was deemed to be a wealthy man.

Indeed, his life course was in this time a path of suffering, but fate had at least paved it with gold and silver pieces. Admittedly, the leading fisherman Hinrich Bull had provided his son-in-law with no further support. Only Stöffe Rütebusch's prediction had nevertheless been fulfilled. Already the inclusion in the propertied fishing family had sufficed to secure the young married man every benefit on the side of the boat owners and smoke houses, and Theder's unrelenting industry had done the rest ...

Affluence and security increased in the newly founded house. Only something did not want to attune itself, peace and contentment. The giant had surely courted with everlasting, never tiring patience at first for affinity, and, when this was curtly and definitely denied him, at least for the esteem of Durtig-Sophie. Only, the man worked so restlessly that as massively as the work grew and swelled under his industrious hands, as much as he towered up money and valuables in his home, Durtig-Sophie did not lose the cold, contemptuous expression in her features, and her dark eyes followed the activity of the giant more and more indifferently and impassively.

"Well, then, esteemed Mr Wasmund, then you must just try it with something else," the scissor grinder suggested one day. His wheel had rung out the warning right before the cottage:

Hurry, hurry, hurry,
Scurry, scurry, scurry.

And Durtig had angrily slammed the window shut. Then the returning giant joined his former mentor there during the midday break, sat down on the cart, and began unveiling, faltering and reluctantly, the secret of his suffering. The club-footed man listened attentively. Then he scratched embarrassedly behind his ears, tore open his toothless mouth, and as he had his raised foot describe all sorts of hieroglyphics in the air, he whispered importantly in the ear of his sunken student, "Theder, pay attention. It is of the greatest importance to you, what my most faithful subservience will have the honour of sharing with you now. You have namely, to say it with respect, started off wrongly up to now with womanhood. You believed in thoughtfulness? Eh what, there you put yourself in darkness. There are two things for which women have respect. Firstly for masculinity with blows of the fist, and gentle rebukes to the back. And for those with whom that does not work, like for example with you and your revered wife Durtig, then just the second main point alone helps. But that is not certain to help. I mean namely that of gifts. The women, esteemed Mr Wasmund, have something in common with mice — they both all want to smell bacon, and if you place the bait in the right place, then they are caught and even whistle the most beautiful songs too. Consider that, Mr Wasmund. I will provide you out of pure friendship with golden rings, garters, corsets, lipstick, and charming shoes."

Hurry, hurry, hurry,
Scurry, scurry, scurry.

***

On the evening of the same day, Theder Wasmund offered his wife two gifts.

It was a wonderful reddish summer evening. Dark golden shadows were weaving about the rooves and trees, whilst the moon already floated bright and limpid in the deep, full, evening blue firmament. The evening wind wafted gently and drove fervent red summer threads before itself.

And the young wife was peering out at these sparkling threads as she now leant relaxing out the window to play musingly with her red plaits. Today she had been married a year. What a dull, dreary, lonely time. Even the wish which had lived strongest in her, the lust for revenge, all started to become more indifferent and meaningless to her. She breathed deeply and was almost startled by her own sigh.

Then she saw the giant man who was her husband creeping cowering and timidly into the house. Strange how low he held his head. Only today did it occur to her. Was he perhaps also suffering? She clenched her fists. But pity, no, she felt no pity for him. May he calmly rot and perish. He was a bad fellow who had been hired by her avaricious parents to weed out by the roots the little goodness which blossomed in her. As she thought over this, a shadow fell into her room, and the giant stood behind her as tightly and as closely as hardly ever before in all this long time. With his crude fists, he stretched something out towards his wife, without a word, and blinking.

Just look, what did it mean? Should there perhaps be a new spitefulness? No, no, even for that, Theder, the only genuine and true Theder, was too stupid.

She threw her head back imperiously, and as she placed her right hand strongly at her side, she burst out defiantly, "What have you brought?"

"Oh, nothing at all, wifey. I have merely brought something with me. See here, a beautiful, big hand mirror with which you can see your face right properly when you are combing your hair. Or so that you can laugh into it, for that all hasn't been for a long time. Look, wifey, and here I bring you also a red coral necklace. It is to put around your white neck, and there is not one like it in all of Trent, as Stöffe Rütebusch tells me."

But Durtig-Sophie was listening attentively, "So?" she asked, shrugging her shoulders, whereby she snapped her fingers a little, "does your friend say that? Such a clever man must understand that. But what else now?", she continued more vehemently.

"Eh, wifey, it is actually our anniversary today."

Then the young wife creased her forehead grimly, and her dark eyes directed themselves dark and inquiring at the man. This stealthy look seemed to want to fathom something important and long awaited, "And you have nothing further to say to me?", she said, restraining herself.

"Me, wifey?"

The giant was already at an end again. The unaccustomed closeness of the redhead had already robbed him anew of all consideration and any deliberation. God, God, if he could only suggest something good and fitting now. Only, he stammered loudly, half to himself, "No, wifey, I don't know. I don't know at all what you mean. Stöffe Rütebusch told me though — —"

He did not get any further, for Durtig laughed brightly and dismissively, then she threw the window open with a wild motion, and now — the giant instinctively floundered and grasped at his hairy face — now she threw the mirror and necklace with all her strength onto the village street.

The glass then clattered and splintered loudly.

"So", she hereupon suggested quite coldly and calmly, and even her breathing seemed to be as regular as ever. "Now carry the junk back to your friend and tell him also how very pleased I was. Make it quick."

A minute later, you really did see how the young fisherman gathered his treasures in the last red of evening. He was already so shattered and beaten down.

***

Only, this last blow, this lasting, drilling, all consuming adversity threw the dulled disposition of Theder Wasmund completely off the rails.

From that day on, the paralysing conviction lay on him that every zeal, every bit of attention would not help him. Where he could actually seek release, deliverance, and salvation, his awkward mind could not guess. It must change though. Lord and devil, change! He could not endure this life any longer. It had become a burden for him, a poisonous potion. And suddenly he felt only the one impregnable desire to kill off his own gigantic nature, and to seek for some low-down forgetfulness before his stabbing pains.

From that day on, Theder Wasmund, the only genuine, true Theder Wasmund, encamped just in the village tavern, drank, swore, and gambled, and threw his money, that sourly obtained, worn-out money, with lunatic abandon into the muck. It was hardly calculable as to what incoherent plan of destruction his unspent nature was forfeiting itself on.

When Stöffe Rütebusch now wheeled his cart through Trent to forecast the weather for his best customers, as this belonged to his traditional duties, then he tended now also to mix with a certain mysterious wantonness the name of the giant Theder in his pronouncements.

He thus spoke to the Parish Councillor of Trent, "Revered Magistrate of Trent, commendable Director of Police. Your potato fields are surely parched at the moment and dry as the skin of my hundred and four year old grandmother Hanne Äcker, who had the honour of being permitted to peel the potatoes for the emperor Napoleon, but I tell you, Mr President, in two days your fields will be as completely drunk as Theder Wasmund, my only genuine and true Theder Wasmund, who does nothing else but drink a pint of beer with a quarter litre of cognac in it. Theder is namely the most extreme of gourmets. Hurry, hurry, hurry."

And for Hinrich Bull, who went around during this period constantly in barely restrained fury and inner rage, the scissor grinder uttered obligingly and naively, "Esteemed patron. You ask about the dog days? Well, they will be uncertain and fluctuating like your stooped son-in-law Theder Wasmund, when he has the honour of sitting for a leech in a puddle. For this very prospective and slow-moving man does that for his inner cooling off. Hurry, hurry, hurry! Have you blunt scissors perhaps? With my own you can cut an ox through the middle."

But something strange also happened during those days. When the esteemed fisherfolk could not restrain the inner indignation anymore, and began needling and lamenting in the home of their daughter that, "He is a rogue, we always said it — a dawdler — a drunk. What? He wants to gamble away our money here?" — then Durtig almost always burst from her chair furiously, and quite against her custom, she set about the defence, "What do you want here? Did I come to complain to you? Are not both our boats outside? And have I desired for anything? We live here as it well suits us, and ask after no man. So, take note of that!" ...

On the evening of the same day on which this happened, Theder Wasmund sat in the humble, whitewashed bar of the village tavern. He crouched quite alone, had his tousled head propped on his giant fist, and stared gloomily out the window. Far away over the currant hedges and resplendent green meadows, towards where the blue sea undulated. Today a moment of special deliberation had come over him, for see, the strangest thing had taken place. His means of numbing was not working anymore. His robust nature had also accustomed itself to the colourful wonder of alcohol. And now he sat there, and misery crouched opposite him and spat in his face. Exactly like his wife had spat at him that time.

And misery spoke to him, "So, my boy, now you are finished. You have wasted your money away and drunk away your manhood. Now report yourself to the poorhouse. Or, if they won't take you there, look, then I have something even better. See here, a rope. And if you don't even merit that, I will be generous, I gift it to you."

Then Theder Wasmund roared out. The rope swayed so distinctly before him that he stretched his hand out to grasp it. His giant body floundered as he now staggered away.

Yes, yes, something was howling in him. Follow the advice. You cannot do any better with yourself anymore.

And misery toddled behind him, slapped him on the neck, and cried, "Make it quick, you rogue."

Then the giant had lost the last power over himself. He ran so that the sweat broke out on himself, and did not stop before he had reached with a few powerful strides the loft room of his cottage.

Quite right — there — yes, there the same rope he had just seen hung down from the beam. Strange, it was exactly the same. He let the rope run through his calloused hands in astonishment and delighted that the line was so white and clean, "Dear Father in heaven", he said in complete confusion to himself. "I don't know anything else now to do with myself. And now don't be angry with me either for this last way out."

But what was that? His eyes were already darkening, or was the image which appeared before him physical and real? The giant stared before himself. No, truly, there, only a few steps from him, there the red head of his wife rose from the trapdoor, and her dark eyes sparkled and flickered for a moment fearfully up at him.

"What are you doing here?", she called out loudly, and her voice broke against the empty walls a few times. At the same time, her hands stroked up and down her skirt a few times.

Only, the giant almost did not recognise the living around him anymore, "Me, wifey?" he repeated dully, as his fists, following the last strong urge, slung the white rope hastily about his neck, "Me, wifey? Eh, I'm merely just —".

The next moment, however, the horrified woman had torn the rope from him.

"Are you lacking something?", she then whispered hoarsely.

The man shook his head without understanding.

"But you are surely tired?", she burst out in chasing haste, as if she must not grudge herself any more time. "Come, come down — why do you have such a red head? — You are getting a fever."

Then she clamped his hand firmly, and it was roaring, humming, and thundering so strangely behind the giant's forehead that he let himself be drawn down the steep ladder unresistingly by Durtig-Sophie. Step by step.

"Wifey," he just murmured to himself, "now I'm sitting high up on a mast, and the storm is beating about my ears."

Straight afterwards, his burning hot body rested on a bed, and it was surely only an accident that Durtig-Sophie had designated her own bed for that, in the little room with the sloping ceiling which her husband had not entered again since that first evening.

And then — what a fortune — then the familiar song rang in her ears unexpectedly from the street:

> Hurry, hurry, hurry,
> Scurry, scurry, scurry,
> Grinder turning fresh and plain,
> Make the knife sharp again,

The young woman tore the window open, "Stöffe, I beg you, come up!"

And when the clubfooted man hesitated before her, she tore out, and pulled full of impatience at his dirty brown vest.

"Don't you see, your friend, Theder Wasmund, wants to die."

The scissor grinder struck both his hands together in genuine horror, he forgot completely all the rules of his compliments book, and began feeling the giant body with fumbling fingers.

Durtig-Sophie shook him again, "Is it coming to an end?", she cried in complete forgetfulness. "He must not — I still want to know something — he must tell me something — help him —".

Only, the scissor grinder had already taken a pair of massive brown plasters from his fathomless vest pocket, now he was intricately folding them together, cutting them with a fine pair of scissors to stick them in the end on the soles of both the recumbent man's feet.

"Revered Madame Durtig," he whispered at the same time, half to himself, "if Stöffe Rütebusch had not entered the venerable house at the most vital moment, then your husband would have — to state with respect — made acquaintance with a small stroke. But Stöffe Rütebusch possesses the sought-after remedy. You must know in fact, the Hamburg senate produced it itself, and had it cast out into the world by the well-disposed scissor grinder. For anyone else a hard taler, but for Theder Wasmund, out of real friendship, 25 pfennigs. Hurry, hurry, hurry. — Forgive me, that is just a habit of mine. And now I will help you wait."

Then the woman asked him if he might sit outside the door, for, because of the question which hovered on her lips, she wanted to be left alone with the very ill man. Whistling and making faces, the clubfooted man hobbled out.

But Durtig-Sophie settled down at the bedside, and as she took the hand of the groaning man in her own, she bent down, and cried loudly and despairingly, "Theder, have you something to say to me?"

But the giant did not stir. He lay stretched out, kept his eyes shut fast, and only dim red shivers chased over his wrecked, boyish face.

"My God," the waiting woman murmured in a low voice, "I do not hear it anymore."

Thus hour went after hour. The moon had long ago climbed over the roof, and now filled the room with that silver flood before which the giant had once shaken so. And see, even now the uncertain beams seem to call awake mysterious life in the outstretched man.

Just then Durtig-Sophie had opened the little window so that the night wind could bring coolness to the man lying there. At this moment, the giant began speaking with his eyes closed. He awkwardly folded his hands over his chest and began. It sounded as if he were gently singing, "Wifey."

"What is it?"

"Wifey — I am now above."

"Above, Theder? Where are you?"

"Oh, wifey, if I knew that. But I am light. And now hear what I have to say in finishing. I don't know either how it has come to me so suddenly. But I think in my stupid mind that the dear angel children that I hear singing around me have surely entered it. Quite distant, quite softly. Do you not hear it too, wifey? Dear God must surely have forgiven me, and now you forgive me too."

"What do you mean, Theder?", Durtig-Sophie murmured, and her eyes widened to an eerie brilliance. "What do you mean?"

But the giant had already gone away again, "But — but," he said quite seriously, "you, dear God in heaven, you know it, Theder Wasmund was a great rogue. That you also first told him today in Möller's tavern. Theder Wasmund was so bad and greedy that he wanted to buy the highest of all in this world. A heart, a human heart.

But Stöffe Rütebusch knows also quite well that I understood none of that at all. Too bad, now I understand it. And now I am sorry, oh, so bitterly sorry, but still more for Durtig. What will surely become of her now? — What will — what will?"

What was that scream?

It sounded so loud, so penetrating, and yet full of liberated, inner jubilation, so that the scissor grinder, who had paid homage to a little sleep outside on his chair, had to stick his head in the door disconcertedly. "Most agreeable, lovely woman ...?", he wanted to spray out just then from his toothless mouth, but the much travelled man was seized by far too strange a picture. Durtig-Sophie lay before the bed on her knees, and was pressing her cheek and the red splendour of her hair into the slack hand of the unconscious man.

Indeed only for a second, for then she springs quickly and decisively up. Only, this passing moment suffices for the experienced man.

"Stöffe," Durtig asks proudly, and imperiously as always, "will he get better?"

"Better, lovely redhead?" — No, Stöffe Rütebusch, the court scissor grinder to the Tsar of Russia, can no longer constrain his wild triumph, and the joy over his being able to submerge his brown eyes so deeply into the heart of the person despising him, he can no longer constrain his wantonness.

"Better, heart-winning, princely redhead? I tell you, Madame Durtig, you do not know at all how much more handsomely. And if you want to comprehend me rightly in your pleasing mind, then you need merely always think of my handy wheel down there. For precisely the stone which grinds the knife in the end most purely and durably, it sprays the wildest sparks at me and often burns the grip in my hand. But it turns out good in the end only if the material is reputable. For it comes down to this, Madame Durtig. And if you perhaps have in a year a small child's cutlery to grind, for you it will be free, from purely well-disposed respect. — Madame Durtig, I have the honour."

THE BIRD PHOENIX

"No," said the old crippled first mate Bob Vatge, who always crouched on a thick bundle of ropes on board the brown Dutch ferry, so to watch out from there for whether us loitering boys did not perhaps take the beautiful cherry-red slices of cheese for our own — for we considered this sort of freebooting to be absolutely honourable and imitation worthy — "no," he said as he shook his head disapprovingly, "you just must not steal."

"Eh what, such a piece of cheese, Bob. Look, merely a bit from the edge here. The Bible does not once forbid that."

"Regards that," he countered, "the Bible is all the same to me. For me, it is merely because of the bird phoenix that you don't take a bite."

"What do you mean?", I stuttered, quickly put my theft aside, and, as I propped my elbows on my knees, I looked insistently at him, "Phoenix? That's the miraculous bird from Arabia."

"May be," Bob Vatge replied quite calmly, "that he lived there earlier. But now he lives here in the Domstraße. And he is the thieves' bird."

"Oh," I dared once more to object, "but you're only imagining that surely? Right?"

"So?", Bob threw back contemptuously, "you think that, my boy? Well, then something tasty can yet be made of you. But so that I am not at fault for your running in complete cluelessness to your green ruin, I want to enlighten you as to the facts. Then you will notice how the bird phoenix is behind every theft like the pike is behind every school of herring. And afterwards you can still do what you like. Stealing or even remaining honest. They are both very meritorious and sustain their man. And now pay attention!"

***

Ante Dauch, old stingy Ante Dauch out there in Vörgelsund, could not sleep. As much as she also tossed about in her narrow bed, which was screwed into the wall in the corridor behind her grocer's shop, as much as she also tossed about on her blue and white checked pillows, it did not help her at all, her rigid, grey eyes remained open. Sometimes it ran like a fire over her bony limbs, for she only ever had the sheets washed once a year. From modesty. For people must not become addicted to throwing money about. And then she had to straighten up again to listen.

"Pay attention — no, no, pay good attention, Ante. Is that really the old south-south-easter which wails thus in the cracks and before the door? Or is someone not breaking and filing at the shop's lock? — God in high heaven, today a drum of mineral oil as well as a new store of salted herring came in. — Maties." — Ante does in fact know very well that the fish do not belong to this distinguished grade, but she calls them so. — If someone would now be so godless and creep into the narrow, little shop? The herring barrel — full of maties — stands right by the entrance. And if someone would then take away five, six — oh dear, absolute Father — or even eight or ten of the beautiful fat creatures! — Certainly, the ropemaker Radvan from next door would surely take a chance on it. The miserable man has not worked at his stool for all of six weeks. For you could hear that work quite clearly. And if he then — — "Huh!", she started in cold fright, "something is creeping next door."

Her fingers trembled.

No, no, this time she heard it quite distinctly. Something was clattering about inside. Quite obviously, the ropemaker Radvan wears wooden clogs. He has thus already gotten in. With a hoarse rattle, Ante lit the candle stump. God, God, such a tallow candle is now so expensive. How can you merely act in such a way sinfully against a poor grocer's widow who nourishes herself pitifully!

In a long shirt which hung loose about her limbs, and with the candle held in front of her, the shaking woman crept thereupon to the shop door. The candle threw wondrous shadows on the brown beam, and leapt and scurried strangely over the long, wrinkled countenance of the creeping woman. Now she peered with bated breath through the little round glass window of the shop.

Nothing. — — Everything empty. The herring barrel still stood at the entrance. And a drop occasionally plunged from the mineral oil drum through the wooden spigot into the tub placed below.

Tick — tick — bot — bot.

"It's good," Ante Dauch suggested, exhaling, "that I merely dreamt it. And the people here are all honest." With that she wanted to shuffle back to bed. But then — then — — oh, heavenly Father, it is thus true — then something was scratching with pointed nails over the wood of the entrance.

In dull fear, Ante Dauch whispered, "Huh — who is there?"

Outside it scratched more vigorously, "Yes, it's me — your sister Rike. Open up quick, Ante, it's not going well for me!"

"What? Rike, you? — Is it possible? — I thought you were washing things at the teacher Kleppien's?"

"Yes, yes, all that later. I beg you as my sister, let me in."

"Quite well, but I have already given you your monthly support — oh, all that money. Do you want perhaps, now in the night, something again from me, a poor, ill woman?"

"Oh Ante, I am so much sicker. Satan is consuming my living body. He sits on my soul, and rides around on it."

"What? — What? — One second!", Ante Dauch called out and delicately gathered her shirt as she skimmed past the herring barrel. But the extraordinary illness of her sister excited the sympathy of the shopkeeper more than she herself confessed.

"If the devil rides around on you, then come in," she relented, coughing, "come in, sister, what's wrong with you?"

With that she drew back the great crossbar, and turned the rusty key. The green door opened creakingly, a wind gust from the sea swept in, and the skirts of the woman waiting outside wafted and rustled.

"Oh God — oh God, how he presses on my poor soul!", the little withered and wizened figure now whimpered, squeezing into the shop to immediately settle down trembling and clattering on the narrow bench by the sales counter. She had placed a basket on the red floor at the same time. "Eh, eh, he is cutting my heart with a bread knife."

Truly, it is a wondrous picture which both the aged women offer now. The one, wizened and tall, in the shirt behind the shop counter, the other before it, hunched up and wet through, in floundering despair.

But between them both is the flickering candle.

"Oh sister, sister," the guest wails, as the woman shakes the drops from herself, "give me a Hamburg plaster quickly so that I can stick it behind my neck against the unrest and devilry."

Here Ante Dauch twists her long, wrinkled countenance in shock. "Do you mean for free?", she would like to refuse.

But the nocturnal visitor, in abrupt haste, as if not a minute more could be lost, throws a groschen piece onto the shop counter. And when the solicitous sister has now sought out the brown, circular plaster, it is stuck by Rike Drewelow in wild haste to the back of her thin, emaciated neck.

"Oh sister, sister, how it goes with me!", the small, wizened creature wails anew at the same time.

"Well, then tell me though!", the older sister urges in her shirt as she seeks to warm her long fingers by the flame of the candle, "It's late — and I'm freezing."

"Well — well, you're freezing, oh, and the devil is boiling genuine, glowing pitch inside me. — Oh, my dear, good sister, you know my blessed husband tended always to say that the evil surely sat in me when I had to peer at other people's possessions. And two years ago, they put me away for six weeks because the merchant Guhlen had found his silver snuff box in my cupboard. Quite accidentally. I could not do anything about it. It was just there. And so it always goes with me."

"Yes, yes, but what brings you today?", Ante Dauch interrupted impatiently as she pushed her upper body in the loose shirt across the shop counter, "Have you found something again today?", she added avidly.

Rike nodded, and wrung her hands sobbing, "What wouldn't I?", she wailed soundlessly, "the devil leaps about in my insides. Think, sister, where that takes me. There I was today washing at the teacher Kleppien's, who married the rich widow, and who is so forgetful. Oh

God, why is he just so forgetful? Why? — Look, and then he has his birthday tomorrow, and now he receives today a hundred mark note sent by an old aunt for it."

"A hundred — marks — —?", Ante tossed in-between, and her bony fingers began avidly counting on the table top, "did you see it yourself?"

"What wouldn't I? — The devil is behind it that he must always show me such things. See, I was just in the room, and because Mrs Kleppien takes everything away from her husband usually, he — as he was now alone with me — stuck the blue note — oh, such a beautiful blue note it was — in the old beer mug up on top of the cupboard."

"Well, and —?", Ante urged, her sharp eyes rising to a shimmer in the reflection of the candle like those of an owl, "have you perhaps already snatched it?"

There Rike shook her head in despair. "No, no, that is just it. The devil was not so strong in me yet. But I must constantly think about it. Always of the old yellow beer mug with the nickel cover on top. Oh sister, and if the Hamburg plaster does not draw the evil out of me, then I don't know what will happen."

"But it will draw it out!", Ante commanded enraged, "I will gift another to you. Then it will certainly help. And now go to bed so that it can take effect. Be quick, for I don't want to house such unholy things in my fine and upright business. Good night!"

With these words, she shoved her visitor inconsiderately and powerfully out onto the village street, and as she placed the heavy crossbar over the door again, she heard how her sister whimpers outside went further and further away, "Oh, how it burns, how it tears. A person cannot endure it for long. No, that you can't."

***

What a shock! As Ante lay again on her blue and white pillows, she noticed with gnawing dismay that Rike's devil had remained behind. Yes, yes, she saw it quite distinctly sitting on the chair by her bed, right on her scarlet petticoat. And the devil took a wad of tobacco, spat a few times, and then growled with a gently seething voice which burned in her ears like pitch:

> Julie, Julie, Julie,
> You are a dumb beast,
> Julie, Julie, Julie,
> You never learn to live.

"Oh, why?", Ante Dauch asked, whereby she crawled down until the covers were up to her eyes.

"Well, why?", the devil thrust again, as his red coal-like eyes flashed at her grimly, "Why? Are you not a poor, industrious woman?"

"That is so — that is so."

"And have you ever seen a hundred marks together?"

"No, no, how shall I have? How shall I merely?"

"But you want surely to wait until your sister Rike scoops it for you? She understands such things."

"Yes, what doesn't she want? — What doesn't she want? But if the teacher notices something now?"

"Eh, for that reason you can rest easy, old Ante. He has never noticed anything yet. And does he not have his birthday tomorrow? And will not many people come there? And can you not also congratulate him?"

"Yes, yes — but now though," Ante Dauch objected, rolling about bathed in sweat.

"What?"

The devil sprang up, went under the top cover with his claws, and nipped Ante on the big toe so that she screamed out. "What?", he blustered, "you want to still object here? On the spot, say now yes or no."

"Yes, yes, I want to!" Ante cried feebly, "I want to do it from pure obedience. Just so that the nipping of my toe should stop."

"That is your luck," the devil soothed her. Then he snuffed out the candle, drank something from his flask, and finally climbed slowly up the chimney.

"Oh, but that is terrible!", Ante whimpered behind him.

***

Only, the devil remained a real man. After two days in fact, Ante Dauch sat happily excited before the box of her shop till, and stroked her long spidery fingers tenderly over a new hundred mark note.

"It possesses the number 601 025 d," she murmured at the same time raptly to herself, "that the old fool of a teacher would not have noted down. But I will write it down. So, here it stands. And now someone shall come."

But look, someone is coming nonetheless. And this one was still much mightier than the devil, for it was the bird phoenix who now lives at 24 Domstraße. But he came flying quite peculiarly, namely with the post. And it happened in the following way.

"Wife, wife!", the tall teacher Kleppien rushed on this day agitatedly to his wife, who was just then cleaning the schoolroom up a little because she had plucked a geese in there that afternoon. "Wife!", the teacher cried, and he waved a large letter with blue seal triumphantly in the air, "Wife, you always said it, dear woman. You maintained that I get involved in too many things which bring nothing in, and which do not work together with each other. For example, with my beekeeping, and with the archaeological research. And then I would have my coin collection, and the census-taking, and the chairmanship in the Christian Teachers' Association, and the issuing of the circulating library. But wife, dear Anna, it is all nothing at all. But this here which I am holding up now, it will make me a rich man. And then it's also something cultural, and something beneficial which behooves my status. Look, wife, I don't want to pride myself on it, but a certain feeling of pride steals up on me when I am now permitted to share with you that the Phoenix, the great association Phoenix, has entrusted me here for our Vörgelsund with the general sales of its burglary and theft insurance. Well, wife, what do you say to that? Is that now something useful and lucrative or not?

Only, Mrs Anna Kleppien did not once turn her blond head to the enthusiastic man. She calmly swept the down together, and just tossed back coldly and calmly over her shoulder, "And how does it stand with the hail insurance which you have had in the past year? Stupid thing. More likely you won't bring a single taler home, better that I don't say a word to this rubbish."

"Anna, dear Anna!", the teacher cried reproachfully, "don't be angry with me, but you are missing the verve and the idealism so important for such a question. This here means something quite different than hail. Such a policy confers on the person, as it states in the prospectus, the certainty of a reassured disposition, and frees them from mistrust. And such a great and beautiful thing should not be turned to account? No, Anna, I am going now straight into the village with it, and you shall see that people will be generally delighted with it."

"Wonderful," Mrs Anna continued sweeping unconcerned, "but this evening the stupid bird story will be sent back."

The teacher found himself already on his way down the street. "Ridiculous," he murmured to himself in striding onwards, "even the best women seem to lack the mind for the more abstract things. This time I will prove it to her. But to whom should I probably turn first? Let me see. Forrr it is clear though that for such a readiness, a certain imagination is called for. Hm, would the baker Ratz be the right man? But he must by profession remain awake all night with his assistants. With him the danger of a break-in equates thus to zero. Or should perhaps — —?"

As he was thus meditating, he wandered straight past the shop of Ante Dauch, and look, Ante sticks her wrinkled head at the same moment out the small, barely foot-high side window with the green panes. But as she became aware of the teacher, she seemed suddenly to dip down to disappear back into the dark of the shop. Only, she was a polite woman, she pondered to herself, and smiled at the passerby as fondly as if her sweet-and-sour countenance allowed her some liberty, "Hello, Mr Kleppien," she began, "all good on the way? — Yes?"

The teacher paused, and was surprised. Strange, this woman had changed very much to her advantage. How considerate it was that she had congratulated him yesterday on his birthday. And today now again this polite address. Certainly, Ante Dauch must have felt a sort of natural goodwill for the teacher.

"Lord, how would it be —?", it suddenly twitched through his mind, "how would it be if this shop-woman — —?"

Without further consideration, he strode up unexpectedly to the open window, and after he had doffed his hat respectfully, he began in serious earnest, "Mrs Ante Dauch, may I perhaps speak for a few minutes on a matter very important to you?"

"Me? — Me?", Ante cried abruptly and grasped at the window crosspiece.

"Don't be frightened," the teacher responded, to some extent confused by this abruptness, "but you can be convinced that for you — hm — you will have after out conversation completely recovered the security of your temperament."

"My security?", Ante had meanwhile turned ashen, "Not out here — before all the people!", she burst out hoarsely. "What you have to say to me, teacher, with me — in the shop."

"Certainly — certainly, that may also lead to the goal much quicker."

And after he now sat opposite her in the dimly dark, frosty space, he overcame the eerie feeling that Ante's rigid eyes were causing him, and decided to attack his opponent boldly head on.

"Mrs Ante Dauch," he began, as he turned his hat to and fro hastily, "you know that honesty is thought to be on the decrease in the world. Can you imagine that there would also be with us — in Vörgelsund — certain entities who are not capable of overcoming the desire for the belongings of their neighbours? Can you imagine that?"

Ante Dauch sat entirely rigid. She just pressed her hands to her wizened breast, and the whites of her eyes could barely be seen. "Oh, the temptation — the temptation!", crept hoarsely from her throat.

Mr Kleppien felt that he was understood.

"So it is," he uttered very satisfied, "I knew straightaway that you would be a rational woman and provide me with little fuss."

"Yes, that surely, but what do you desire from me now?"

"Please, follow me just for another step!", the teacher demanded, settling down with ever increasing comfort into this beautiful speaking part. "If we now assume someone would be so reprehensible and steal from you wares with a value of — of two hundred marks."

"No, only a hundred," Ante Dauch fended with raised hands, "no more."

"Well good, that also suffices. Would you now not leave every stone unturned to put that matter right again, to make it unhappen in a sense?"

Ante Dauch opened her eyes wide, and raised her right hand as if she wished to lift up a handkerchief to wipe away the cold sweat from her forehead. "To make it unhappen?", she stammered with dry lips. "Eh, eh, what would I not want to? But how do you do that, teacher? Oh, please, explain me that."

The teacher was stirred. He would not have considered such an affectionate embrace of his social philosophy to be possible with this otherwise so cold woman. Hence he enthusiastically rose, and tapped his listener encouragingly on her stiffly erect back.

"So nothing easier than this, my dear Ante Dauch," he continued his lesson rapturously. "You simply undersign this policy, and engage yourself perhaps for the period of five years."

"Five — years — is at stake?" Ante murmured, slumping down.

"Yes," the teacher concluded in great triumph, "and you fix all that then with a hundred marks. You will admit that this is the utmost that is able to be offered to you. Are you agreed to that?"

"Eh, eh, nothing else surely remains to me. And I thank you many times, Mr Kleppien. And here — oh God, look — this is the hundred mark note. But tell me just one thing for heaven's sake; does nothing more follow from this now?"

The teacher Kleppien intricately folded the money up, but then he straightened up proudly, and in full consciousness of his proven worth to the bird phoenix, he replied as nobly as possible, "I affirm to you, dear Mrs Dauch, that this matter is dealt with here once and for all. My character hopefully acts as guarantor to you for anything further. Right? And now thank you for the prompt settlement, Mrs Dauch, and be assured once more that you will not have to complain over the noblesse of the Institute."

A minute later, the teacher Kleppien could be seen erectly striding down the village street in radiant sunshine. Ante Dauch, however, watched after him through the tiny green glass window until she finally, still shaken with inner horror, burst out, "Yes, yes, you are right in that. I have nothing to complain about the noblesse. How noble the way was by which the accursed note was taken off me again. Nothing once compares with an educated man. But who is at fault for the whole business? Who? My sister Rike. And that is why I am depriving her of support from now on."

***

"So, that is the story of the bird phoenix," the first mate Bob Vatge concluded, "and hence I advise you not to give in to theft. For this famed bird notices it immediately. And alongside his cleverness, the highest judge of the law also stands there as a white tallow candle. — So, consider that."

THE FLYING DUTCHMAN

And then — and then — like a blue bolt of lightning, it travels through the dark, smoky bar to wander about the dark wooden walls so angularly. And then — a penetrating scream, a fall, a clatter, a brawl, a dull, despairing groan which nobody understands, nobody wants to interpret. Then the torn-down lamp, thrown to the ground, goes out, a fume rises, and everything becomes still.

Only the same scream once more from a distance, the same groan, the same sobbing as if from a martyred soul unburdening itself.

The drops run over the small steps.

Tick — tick — tick. It could also be a clock, it remains so indistinct.

And then suddenly a kick against the barricaded door, vigorous knocking, the reflections of a police lantern, and the regular, alarming words heard so often, "Open up — in the name of the law!"

****

A summer night is spreading itself over the green Pomeranian bay. Everything near and far seems to be hung with these airy, floating, light green veils. They float down from the silent groves which enclose the still water in wide arcs, they are wound about the large, crimsonly dawning moon, they dance along on the enormous expanse of water, greenly evaporating and blurring again, and, quite far off in the small mariners' village, they draw across the rooves and empty streets, always skipping, interweaving, a tender, elusive spirit folk who would like to announce something which we men do not understand, "Wake up — wake up, it is there, joy or sorrow — or both — who knows, who can fathom it? Who? But we, we know it."

"Grandma", a bright girl's voice encouraged in the dark bedroom of the pilot's cottage, and at the same time, Marik Thurow moved the pillow a little further under the feet of the old woman next to whom she was crouching on a low footstool in the green shimmering darkness. "Grandma", she began anew as she, turning to the low window, began letting down her abundant red hair. "And so our Lord Jesus Christ died on the cross for all of us?"

"Yes, my daughter," it trembled out of the darkness, and the wizened finger of the old grandmother Kase rustled in the yellow pages of the Bible, although she now could not read the holy book at night. But already the fingering was deemed by the pious woman to be curative and refreshing. "Well, my daughter, he left his young, beautiful life for all of us now. And for that we must be thankful to him."

Marik pulled off her rough shoes, and fingered her stockings. Then she stared out into the green clouds of the village street.

"Tell me just one thing, grandma," she finally began anew, "do you think that such a thing is even possible these days?"

The old woman did not understand her, slowly shut the heavy Bible, and hesitated a little. Then she inquired with an audible drawing of breath, "Possible today? How do you mean, Marik?"

Meanwhile the young girl had stood up, and she was now shedding her clothes and skirts with gentle fingers adroitly and almost inaudibly, so that she soon after loomed in her white, innocent linen shirt before the old woman, "Eh, I mean, grandma," she tried again, as she slung her bare arm for a moment gently over the shoulders of her forebear, "such a great goodness which can console all of mankind and make them better, that was surely only possible in such holy times? Do you think that in our times even, a man can redeem others? Since for that, I see it well in my dumb mind, for that you must surely be God's child."

"Yes", the old woman said, and looked rigidly at the white figure. "Such a one must be God's child. And I have not experienced it yet either. But who knows? It would be miraculous though if God's son should have vanished so entirely from the earth. But of that we both know nothing. And that is also a frightening story. And now come and lead me to bed. And you yourself lie down too. For look, the moon is already coming over our roof, and that is the sign that it will soon be turning eleven. Now come, Marik."

With that the old woman rose weakly from her seat, and it was a strange picture, how the young girl now drew the old woman to herself, divesting her piece by piece of her rough clothes to finally lay her in the massive rustic bed in which, according to the custom of the area, enormous white and red checked pillows rested towering over one another.

And when the old woman stretched her wizened limbs comfortably on the pillows, she folded her hands, murmured something, and admonished once more, "Now let that be, my daughter, and don't think anymore of it. As for us common folk, such thoughts are nothing more than pride, and that does not do any good ..."

Boom, it rang out suddenly across the sea.

"Listen", Marik said, and placed her finger to her mouth.

Boom, it went once more, and a slow booming thunder rolled across the expanse.

Old Kase straightened herself again arduously on her pillows, and her ancient mouth chewed back and forth fearfully.

"Is Thomas, my boy, all here?", she inquired, and stroked the covers restlessly with her hand.

"No, grandma, father will be piloting a foreign ship. It's from Holland."

"So?", the old woman murmured, "shall it be?" And after a while, she added half unconsciously, "My blessed one was also from Holland. Good — right good — but ..."

Boom, it thundered once more, and now a bluish glow also twitched over the panes as if it had flashed from the sea.

"They are probably demanding a second pilot," the girl declared, "and now father will also be home soon."

And as she already lay stretched out in her much smaller bed next to her grandmother, she tossed about uneasily, and sent her thoughts incessantly over to the great ship, one much greater than had ever arrived at anchor in this region. What sort of strange men might be on board? Thus it passed through her head. And whether they wore different clothes than us? And whether we will understand them? And whether they will stay here for long?

And she threw herself to and fro for such a long time until her thoughts floated into the realm of dreams. And all that was contradictory came together. The massive ship with a strange prow, but in the middle of it, nailed bloodily to the main mast striving for heaven, the Lord and Saviour from whose side-wound the blood trickled, and whose mouth opened for the words, "I am over all times."

***

Truly, it was the largest ship which had ever dropped anchor in this quiet bay. A five master which was on the way to the Dutch East Indies. Late in the evening, when the red and green signal lanterns were burning on the uppermost yards of the mast, the lights were seen for miles across the flat heath landscape of the coast. Then little flaxen-haired boys surely crouched together in the middle of the fields on the wavy furrows, and Klaus would say to Stöffe, "Look, up there dear God is hanging out his stall lanterns. Look, proper red and green."

And the vessel had to remain lying there perforce for several weeks. An engine defect which could only be fixed by one of the dockyards in the vicinity was being dealt with, and in the meantime a livelier traffic between the ship's crew and the coastal inhabitants emerged by itself.

Hey, those were cheerful days. The Dutch talers leapt and sprang just so through the village lanes, and they already began exercising their strangely transforming effect. Both the taverns in the coastal village of Wisby were no longer empty, and when the well-built Dutch-men, whose low speech you thought you understood and yet did not grasp, turned in their solemn slow na-tional dance in the taverns, then it ran through the women and girls of the place like a wildfire, "Kerstin, did you see what red vests the men had with the shiny talers on them?"

"Yes, and then, Dörthe, the funny long ribbons on their caps, and what sort of forearm-long, white clay pipes were they twisting in their fingers?"

"Yes, and then, thunder of God, you surely noticed the captain with the massive white beard?"

"Would I not? He is the one who in dancing stamped his foot so comically, and whenever he did that, he seized a man lovingly, and kissed him right on the mouth. That must surely be a custom in his homeland."

"Yes, that it must well be. But you want to run along quickly so that the others do not beat us to it, for such a dance, that is something out of the ordinary."

Yes, then they ran in crowds to the strange men, and the round dance turned, and the Dutch folk dances went solemnly through the hall, around to the right, around to the left, and then in the middle, the one leg raised dignified, and clapping the hands.

Clap — clap.

Yes, that was something.

And when you were then red and hot, well then, then just the finest of all occurred. Then the stout, dignified gentlemen revealed red wine and champagne bottles. Indeed nobody really knew where they got this refreshment from, only that you did not need to inquire for long about it with such distinguished foreigners. Pip — pop, the corks banged everywhere from the obstructed nooks and crannies of Möller's tavern, giggling could be heard and coarse-grained swearing, and in the middle of the hall then, the white-haired captain was enthroned with his long billowing, glimmering beard, and held in his lap with dignity the youngest girl who did not really know what to say to all this strange bustle. And the well-built ship's captain only opened his mouth occasionally to let out a short, hollow sounding laugh quite suddenly and abruptly over the audience.

"Ho — ho."

Then the others were frightened for a while, and then the din continued.

Yes, the Dutch period, the people of Wisby still think of it today.

***

"Father," Marik Thurow asked the tanned, broad-shouldered pilot one Saturday evening as he sat with her and old Kase quietly resting on the green bench before the pilot's cottage. "Father, may I not even once see the foreigners?"

At this question, the mariner raised his head, whereby, as if by accident, his look met with that of the old woman, and then he shifted his wad of tobacco a bit to reply quite calmly and coolly, "No, my daughter."

But the old woman nodded and acted as if she wanted to adduce an entirely new viewpoint, but only brought forth, "No, no, my daughter."

"Yes, but, father —".

"I know best", the pilot overruled her, as he gently brushed his knee with his palm, and this time the old woman also added, "No, no, Marik, your father knows best."

After that it went quiet between the three. The sea wind purred about the house, and in both the poplars striving for the sky before the gate, a flock of black starlings sat. They occasionally flapped their wings in dreaming, sometimes a quiet, lost chirp also arose. But over the village street, the full moon floated, crimson and distant, and the wind carried over quite from afar dance music from the tavern.

Cling — cling — plump — plump — trallah. Now Marik quietly rose, and as she leant with her arms on the garden fence, she looked first down the deserted, moonlit village street, to then turn her eyes to the poplars in whose highest branches the flicker of the moon reflected off the black feathers of the starlings.

How it twitched and flashed bluely. And did it not shimmer also like a dark, sparkling bloom in the girl's eyes?

"She isn't crying though?", the pilot and his mother thought almost simultaneously.

Only, Marik shed no tears. She was far too accustomed to being led by the will of her nearest, and what stirred in her soul at that moment unrecognised and dull was only an unapprehended wingbeat of the spirit which was striving out of narrowness and constriction.

But she did not understand that. And half unconsciously, a question about the great ship which still occupied all her thoughts again poured out.

"Will it sail away now soon, father?"

"Yes, my daughter, in a week they will probably clear off. But who knows?" — the pilot seemed to his only child, whom he had usually distanced so strictly from the delights of youth, to be wanting to offer an innocent pleasure. "You know what, tomorrow, on Sunday, the entire crew is leaving the ship, and carrying on their loud existence here on land until late at night. In the meantime, I will allow you to take my boat around the Dutch ship, and look at it from all sides. Would you like that, my daughter?"

Then Marik clapped her hands together, and her eyes flashed. "Yes, father!" she cried, "I would like that." And after a while, she added, "Tell me one thing, what is the great ship actually called?"

"Eh," the pilot suggested as he slowly rose to carry his lamed mother into the house, "it has a funny name which does not actually fit right. It is called 'The Flying Dutchman'. And with this name, something strange once happened a long time ago. But I don't know what exactly either, and it probably has no meaning anymore today. And now go to bed, Marik, and get up again quickly early in the morning."

The daughter promised that. But when she stepped into the house, she could not restrain herself from first springing up once more to the dark loft from where a small circular little window peered out at the sea. Then she rose up on her toes. Deep below her rested the ebbing sea on which it played back and forth like green and black worms which were swallowing each other. And quite far back, there it rose out of the emptiness like a black rock, and three red lights twitched back and forth from it. They bored through the night more and more seethingly and fierily.

My God, Marik thought, as she pressed her fingers to her temples, it looks like burning blood.

And then she quickly shut the round pane, and then scurried with pounding heart over the creaking steps and into her waiting bed. "Good night, grandma", she murmured.

"Sleep well, my dear", it sounded from the other side.

***

It was towards midday.

The last words of the sermon had faded away in the church, and the farewell tolling of the bells was swinging brightly and joyfully over the wide sea. It was glorious how the water spread out today. It lay there like a green mossy carpet gleaming with dew, on which fantastic white water lilies blossomed and sank again. And really, when Marik went over the water in her boat with short, uncertain oar-strokes, she noticed with astonishment how the sea's springtime had enticed over entire clouds of yellow brimstone butterflies which seemed to snatch flitting and playing at the white blossoms.

She raised her eyes and looked up at the radiant sun. Did the day-star not shine and flash like an enormous disc which had become white-hot in the fires of morning and now sprayed down thousands of red sparks which passed through the blue aether and fizzed down into the green water?

And how strange, she hardly needed to move the oars. Driven by an invisible power, her dinghy glided, following a sea current, certain and without faltering. The girl slowly let the oars in, then she bent forward peering, and stroked her Sunday clothes uncertainly, having arranged them with special care today, not knowing herself why.

"Why actually?", she asked herself, since the great vessel which emerged with its giant masts closer and closer and more and more tangibly stood completely deserted according to her father's report. A ship's boy at most might be hanging about on the deserted planks. And then perhaps too — yes, quite rightly — her fine ear had not deceived her, truly, there something barked, sharp and yelping over the calm surface, and now her eyes, accustomed to the sea, also distinguished how a small black dog sprang back and forth hurriedly at the outermost point of the enormous vessel. But otherwise nothing living was to be noted, no clouds of smoke curled up, no men's voices rang out, all the life seemed as if it had wafted away from the great black monster.

Strange, Marik thought, it lies there as though cursed. — And suddenly she is seized by a hidden fear, by an unnameable trickling shivering before the silent colossus which seemed to draw her boat quicker and quicker to itself like the magnetic mountain from the mariners' legend.

What was that? Was a stronger swishing not rising before her boat? Was it really possible that her boat was moving forwards with doubled force? No, no, that could only be imagination, and now it became more and more certain to her in her excited disposition that she no longer possessed any desire anymore to have a close look at this monstrosity of the watery wastes which lay before her so dead and stiff.

"I want to go back", she stammered. "Quite certainly, I want to go home. To father and to grandmother Kase."

And in sudden abrupt fright, she thrust both oars into the water, and began throwing both back in mad, erratic haste.

But is it possible? Great God, what does it all mean? Has she lost the power over her usually so manageable boat? Or is the white, dancing glow of the sun confusing her!?

Floundering and swaying, the boat turns in circles, and now — ah, that was the last — with a sharp jolt, one of the oars sprang from its strap and had already drifted a good stretch from her across the surface before Marik could see what had thereby happened to it.

"No, no, I want to go back, I want quite certainly to go back", she murmured still distractedly as she sprang up in the swaying boat, and stretched out her arms for the vanished oar. But there — where had she had her eyes? — With a dull crash, the boat thrust into something tall, black, towering, and then it lay still and secured. Closely nestled against a dark tarred wall about which the sea stroked and whispered.

The girl sat down quite numbly on one of the seats. In her heart, so much timidity and fear reigned that she hardly dared breath audibly.

What now? Should she remain lying forged here now? Past midday? Until evening? For perhaps as long as until the crew returned drunk and jeering? Incapable of any clear deliberation, she placed her cold fingers over her eyes, and brooded with a dull anxious feeling to herself. But when no sound, no step, and not the slightest sign of life arose from the foreign vessel, she gradually calmed down. Praise God, it seemed quite apparent that the black vessel rested completely deserted, and with this knowledge, she dared to push her boat off anew with both hands. When she again found herself a few steps from the colossus, she peered up furtively. The deck was empty, the masts lonely, nothing, nothing stirred in this deathly Sunday rest, nothing but the small black Pomeranian which sat calmly on the boards, and stared motionlessly at her with its dark eyes. Marik also did not stir. Without admitting it to herself, she entertained a timidity before the staring dark animal.

Thus she may have remained for an hour inactive and dazed in the sparkling light before the black edifice.

But then, it was so entirely strange in a way — the dog had barked, or could the man have been called over by something else? Or did the entirety consist of a delusion like the sun on the sea so often conjures? Marik stared breathlessly up.

See, on the roof of the cabin, a man in a blue sailor's uniform seemed to already have been sitting for some time, his head propped low in his hands, and must have taken in the picture before him for a long time and motionlessly with large dark, serious eyes. And when Marik sent up another hasty glance, she perceived that this man possessed a countenance as if made from pale porcelain, and that his eyes looked so sombre, just like that of the dog at his feet.

The pair goggled at each other incessantly. And the silence on the great ship was preserved and extended.

Only, the fresh, innocent creature could not endure this stretching, heart-clenching remoteness any longer. Besides, her heart was pounding as if she were standing before a definite decision. She had to, had to, and even if it were only to hear her own voice. She straightened up, and placed her hand unconsciously above her eyes, "Oh," she asked, and at the same time, she did not know anymore what she was saying, nor to whom, "oh, help me."

The man on the ship raised his head imperceptibly, although his shaded eyes did not allow any further accord to be recognised.

"My oar has floated away from me", Marik continued more wildly. "Help me get to it again."

The helmsman shook his head imperceptibly.

"No?" the girl repeated uncomprehendingly.

Then the man rose to speak. "No," he said with a deep and yet soft voice, "I may not."

"May I not be helped? May I not retrieve the oar?"

She shook her head quite helplessly, and pressed her hands together.

"Why not?", it poured unconsciously from her.

The man turned his head to her, his eyes took on a dark, dismissive expression.

"Because — because —", he seemed yet to be struggling with himself, but then the clueless innocence of the girl must surely have urged him further than he was himself fond of going; "because," he replied sombrely, "because I have never left the ship in five years."

"For five years?", the half-numb girl echoed in turbid amazement.

"Yes, yes — so it is."

With that he rose again, a clattering was heard, and then he pushed down one of the ship's oars which he threw recklessly and in a wide arc to the girl.

He added not a word more, and when Marik, after she had fished the oar out of the water, once more wanted to turn to him, she perceived only how the stocky figure of the foreigner slowly and without looking back disappeared into a cabin.

Only the black Pomeranian still crouched on the boards, and did not let up following her with his flashing, rolling eyeballs.

Then the abandoned girl suddenly deployed the mismatched oars without thinking, and, like lightning, her boat shot to the shore and her home.

When she had reached the shore, Marik rushed home as if chased.

The image of the lonely vessel, as well as that guest hostile to mankind who guarded it, did not leave her anymore. In dreaming and waking, she constantly heard the dark voice, and even in sleepless night, the lamenting cry rose, "Five years, five long years."

Why? Why surely in all the world? How was such a thing possible? Great God, five years of not touching land? Not seeing its blossoming trees? Not treading its loose crumbs of earth? Feeling no shadows, and not smelling the scent of hay? And never, never stopping off in the houses of familiar people?

Why? Great God, just why?

"Father, are there sailors who may never, not even ever, leave their vessel?"

"No, my daughter, that I have not heard of yet. There surely may be such who have resolved something with themselves. And dear God protects us from these."

"Yes, yes," old Kase added, "there is nothing holy in such."

It remained at that.

And the flushed up thoughts chased and wandered unchanged about the distant, black vessel.

How did it happen that, early the next morning when the sun had barely risen over the blue horizon, how did it happen that the girl was already pushing off again in her boat to the uncanny goal?

How did it happen?

No, no, she does not want to go there. Quite certainly not. Just to let herself be blown a little by the wind, to have a little look. To see the fish leaping and the white herons shooting across the water. Just that, without a doubt just that. How did she also come to look out for a strange vagrant who, as her grandmother said, certainly possessed something unholy? Not seeing land for five long years, dear Jesus, what a terrible torment, what a torturous punishment. Whether he had surely imposed it on himself?

And see, there she notices him already again. With arms thrown down, he stands there, and his dark, eyes, so uncanny to her, seemed to follow every movement of the approaching girl. They examined each other for some time from a distance, silent and wordless. But strangely, why does the man now throw a rope ladder over the side? Is that for her? Oh no, never, she will never set foot on this swaying bridge. For Jesus Christ's sake, she will never dare it at any price. She has not appeared for that reason.

And now — now she is grasping the rope ladder, a short swing, and with a deep sigh which her breast emits quite instinctively, she raises herself slowly and arduously to the deck. Now they stand opposite each other. And again they examine each other, peering for a long time, like two people who have not seen each other since time immemorial, and have finally found each other again.

How strange, she does not know the man at all. And it is almost not unthinkable that she now, following a short imperative wave from him, sits next to him on the flat roof of the cabin? At the same time, the sun beams and flickers numbing on their bare heads. Everything seems like a waking and yet desolate dream.

"No, it is not true", the helmsman begins as he stares at the deck, and scrapes back and forth on it restlessly with his foot. "It is not true", he begins as if he had already answered her question many hours before. "The sailor five years ago in the Dutch tavern in Amsterdam, he did not commit it. How can you believe it? It was merely a coward, a quite common man, one of the many with whom she did business with in her unrestrained nature which she knew to hide so prettily. No, no, you must not have any suspicion on that. You — you — what is your name?"

"Marik."

"Marik — yes, yes, I thought so. No, Marik, he was not the one, that you surely also think. It was an entirely different one, a stupid, unworldly fellow, a man for whom his girl was everything, who thought of nothing but her, for whom her loyalty was higher than heaven, and her love wider than the sea. Yes, yes, they are such silly phrases. Do you remember still the evening, the November evening in the 'White Harbour' in that lane Antjegasse?"

"Me?" She stared at him aghast. "Me? How would I?"

"So — so — that is just me as you must know. Do you really not ponder anymore how the other one, the right one, found her in the corner where she had crept with the coward? And then, it must surely have been a knife — it was not there anymore afterwards. Perhaps it was also a blue bolt of lightning, who can know. But it must have been done. Right? You will bear me out that the god of revenge came down so that the court had to be held without much rhetoric and in daylight tearing. For what stands so close to one must be preserved from utter disgrace. Right? Everything is in order? So it must go. Thus it speaks."

"Yes, yes", Marik murmured numbly, and grasped her forehead in a blurred faint. "It is all just as you say."

"Well, then, you are rational, Marik. But look, how comes it that I find no peace now? How shall I interpret it that it now creeps up behind me on cheerful days, and I must constantly hear the rustle of a long, woman's train? There — there — do you not notice anything? There behind us, behind the centre mast, there it creeps again. Don't shake your head, it is quite certainly so. For see, you must know the girl wore a silk train from all the wages of sin. But I make nothing of that. Ho — ho —, who can appear and say that I am frightened? Over the entire night, I lie with open eyes and speak with her. But frightened? That you surely do not believe, Marik?"

"No", Marik replied, murmuring to herself as she looked at her bloodless hands. "That I don't believe."

"Yes, but now though," he startled her, and grasped his head, "the last thing, look, girl, that I do not dare."

"What? You don't mean though — —?"

"Yes — yes — I mean just that. How is the sea so wide and the ship so empty. I need merely glide down the rope ladder here. Quite simple, nobody will hear it. It would be so still, as if a child were going to sleep. And see, that I do not dare. And why, Marik? Yes, girl, one cannot know, it just is. If up there now, behind the blue clouds, a thundering voice rolls, just as we hear it during a storm when an unending boom rumbles across the sea, without beginning and without end. And if that then asks. Such a single short question through marrow and bone. And if it looks at one with two eyes which are actually red bolts of lightning. What then? Look, Marik, whom do I have then? Who shall help me then? What shall I say then? No, no, I must travel on, ever further, without stopping. Do you understand that?"

She nodded.

Then she hid her head in her hands, and through her fingers in the reflecting sunlight, her glistening tears trickled.

The man wiped the drops away with the rough sole of his boot, "Enough," he said heedlessly, "you cannot help me either, although ..." He interrupted himself. "Go home," he burst out hastily, "go home where all the others live. See, it is dragging again, and rustles behind me. There I know all the news. And I am not frightened of it. Not of it. Go!"

He stretched his hand out, and obediently, as if there were no rejoinder in this world to his expressed will, the girl climbed down the tottery rope ladder. Inch by inch she went down, but her crying eyes remained directed at him as long as the deck was visible to her.

Then she sought her way home with broad, almost superhuman oar-strokes. Always murmuring to herself, "Yes, yes, it is right, it is certainly all right and good."

***

"What is it with the girl?" the pilot Thomas Thurow asked his old mother in the evening as he was lingering by her bed, "why is she not yet in bed? What is goading her?"

Old Kase moved her head back and forth, and brushed her hand over the covers, "Eh," she said, "I think the girl stands up in the loft before the little window, and looks out at the dark sea."

"At the bay?", the pilot repeated in astonishment, as he scratched behind his ear, "what is she looking for there?"

"Eh, after this and that, but mainly probably after something which is merely present in her thoughts. And that is bad."

"Yes, yes, what didn't she want?", Thomas Thurow thought to agree in a low voice. But at this moment, the door opened soundlessly, and in slipped Marik. She was already walking in bare feet, and was startled when she became aware of her father.

"How goes it, my daughter?" the pilot inquired cautiously. And when his daughter had fleetingly nodded her head, he stroked her hair smoothly, and began speaking to her as gently and comforting as hardly ever before, "Well, you know well, sweet girl, that we are all good here. And man need not know more to feel strong and confident in his position. So, now you know. I don't want to say any more to you."

Then he once more stroked her long ash-blond hair, which already hung down in a pair of heavy plaits, and left the little room with his heavy steps crunching on the sand.

Soon afterwards, the girl also lay outstretched next to old Kase. And it was night around her. Black, impenetrable night, from which she did not know any way out. How her heart hammered. So loudly, so wildly that she thought old Kase must hear it. But the old woman lay quite still and gently snored.

And again Marik pressed her hands to her temples to murmur at the same time those words which she had to speak to herself incessantly on this day, "It is good — it is all good, what he did. Great God, and you, Lord Jesus Christ, if it is a sin, then forgive me, and forgive him, but I don't know anything else."

The hours flew across the land from the church tower. The waking heard it strike one and then two.

Then something quite wondrous happened. But it also had such an improbable effect when it occurred that she knew then that she had been waiting constantly for it.

At the windowpane of the little room, something ticked. It was as if a small piece of gravel had been thrown against the glass.

Listen, what was that voice which called then? Now it rang out once more, "Marik!"

Then it happened about her.

Sleepwalking and yet quite conscious, as if she were drawn along by cords on her arms and feet, and on the other hand again quite happily and voluntarily, she fled through the door. Quite secondarily, she thought to throw a coat over herself. But she otherwise left the little room bare-footed, her full, beautiful arms gleamed bare, and when she now stepped out onto the moonlit village street, the nocturnal sea wind played with the thin linen over her breast.

And there, right before her, in the middle of the deserted street stood the foreign man. He immediately grasped her by the hand as if it were quite natural that this creature had followed his first call. He did not seem to notice her bareness and the entire way she stood before him.

"Marik," he whispered to her, "I have climbed onto land now, for now it has come so far. And I knew straightaway that you must live in this house. And do you know also why I come? I wanted just to tell you that I have now decided. Tonight I will do it. For a person now lives who knows here how much I am frightened of the great court of the world. That is you. And that I don't want."

Then she looked at him quite wide-eyed, and began suddenly stroking his cheek, maternally, tenderly.

The man was startled.

"And I?", she asked quite calmly.

"You?"

With a powerful step, he was next to her, placed his hand heavily on her head, and stared with his sombre eyes into her pale countenance.

"Are you really that which I hardly know, and yet which belongs to me? Is there such a thing? You — you, do you also know what it means to be one with me?"

Again she looked at him entranced, and then a voice spoke from her to which she herself listened because it hardly seemed to belong to her anymore, "But I must do everything. I do not know myself why. And do you see, if I go with you, it seems so clear to me," — here she raised her head and looked confidently up at the golden starry heaven — "He will not refuse the intercession for me. For you surely believe that I have done nothing willingly wrong."

"Yes", he confirmed as he did not let his dark penetrating look leave her anymore. "That is clear. And I will not reject you either. For see, it must surely be all so, otherwise I would not have been so certain in my case, and would have never ever fetched you."

"Were you?" she asked.

"Yes, I was. — For, without you, you see, without you, I would not dare."

See — the loving, cheerful smile again slid about her mouth, and her finger again caressed encouragingly and comforting over his bearded cheek, "Then come," she demanded insistently, "then I will show you everything once more before we go. The fields, and the water meadows to which the grey mists draw. And the reeds by the sea, and all the little houses here behind their ragged orchards. And then, then we will also stop once more before the church door."

"What will we do there?"

"There you shall once more place your hand on my head like before. For I believe that it is necessary so that I can endure what I am carrying out. Now come!"

***

In the grey of morning, a man stepped out of the ancient gods' grove which menaced blackly and darkly over the water. In his arms, he carried a woman, clothed only with a linen shirt, who clung firmly in his arms with face averted. The heavens stretched colourless above them, and only the morning star still sparkled unfaded down on them. "I will turn the wheel to there," the man said calmly. "And when we land, then I know that the blessing remains with us. For after I learnt that God's eternal goodness also still lives on in individuals, then I realised that no court awaited me, but that we will enter quietly and calmly into a silvery eternity, just like the calm water will close over us now. Come, Marik, you carry the key in your hand. Open up!"

And calmly, his burden pressed passionately to himself, he strode onwards. The reeds caressed his hair, the cool seawater climbed up to his chest, and the dim morning waters struck together soundlessly over them.

The firmament arched bluer and bluer, and the morning star stood immovably, in radiant brightness, as if it were a gate through which two souls were just receiving their entrance at this early hour.

BISMARCK

Bismarck

"Good morning, Mr Zacharias Boldt," the tall gaunt shepherd Sturm wished, as he drove his bleating flock with measured step past the low wooden fence of the fat horse dealer. "Good morning, Mr Zacharias Boldt," the shepherd repeated once more thoughtfully, as he leaned a little over the prongs of the fence, for the shepherd of the small North German borough loved neither busyness nor haste, and scorned time. "You feel in good health surely?"

"Yes," Fatty Boldt said, who stood wide-legged at some distance, and with his hands in the pockets of his trousers, in his paved yard. And at the same time, he jingled a little with his heavy golden watch chain, which bounced back from his rotund body with each step. "It's going beautifully for me."

"Good." The shepherd rocked his head. "And yet I come to warn you, Mr Boldt."

This address sounded so solemn and hushed that it would certainly have startled any other citizen and patriarch, or at least made them curious. But Fatty Boldt just twisted his morose, red-stubbled countenance somewhat more grouchily so that countless creases and wrinkles were furrowed into his leather-coloured skin like hundreds of the intersecting drainage ditches which burrow across the brown dirt fields. And then he very coolly said nothing but the one word, "So."

At that he spat indifferently onto his boot.

"Yes," the shepherd Sturm continued, undisturbed by this lack of concern, "I come to warn you. You know the old dealer Daniel Katz there in Wolgast?"

Fatty Boldt nodded. He knew him.

"Well yes, I just met him in the tavern, and there he told a business traveller that he wanted to travel out to you today to tear out a few of the hairs from your beard, Mr Boldt. For he says he had not yet been able to earn anything from you until now. And that may also be true. But today he suggested he would tie you up in your nest. You surely understand? See, and that I wanted merely to announce to you beforehand. For Daniel Katz" — here the shepherd grinned almost imperceptibly to himself — "is a very delicate businessman."

"Does him no help," Fatty Boldt coughed, since the air occasionally ran out from him, "I have a means against it."

"So? What then?"

The horse dealer spat again, and looked very satisfied.

"Bismarck," he responded, whereby he wiped a pair of creases away with his rough hand, well-pleased.

The shepherd stepped back, and raised his blue eyes in astonishment at the other man.

"What?", he wondered, as he tapped his chest lightly with his crook. "I know many means, but I have heard nothing yet of Bismarck. From where do you have it?"

"Eh, my dear shepherd," the horse dealer suggested with great deliberation, "we are not just born yesterday either. And I have learnt Bismarcking from the newspapers, and tend to use it during great and uncommon events — such ones as Daniel Katz is — with beautiful success."

"Ah, so, you probably don't want to let out anything more about what it is?"

"No," the dealer cut him off distrustfully. "No more, for it is my business secret. And now go, shepherd Sturm, I see in fact Daniel Katz coming on his yellow ramshackle carriage. And here I must prepare myself a little for Bismarcking. Adieu!"

"Remarkable," the shepherd thought when he had already moved off a long way in the midst of his flock. "Bismarck must be a very strong means. What is it surely?"

But neither he, nor his learned dog Karo were able to form even just the tiniest idea of this new remedy.

***

Meanwhile tiny Mr Katz had clambered down hurriedly from his carriage, and as he now became aware of the unmoving dealer, who was still staring down as perfectly indifferently and impassively at the puddle-covered ground as if it were especially beneficial to his health to count the uneven cobblestones, Daniel Katz began swinging his old woolly top hat enthusiastically, and skipped so stormily over to the horse dealer that his yellowed, crumpled squire's coat fluttered and rustled in the wind.

"Loyal servant — loyal servant, my dear revered Mr Boldt. How prosperous you look. No, and what a peaceful and amiable look you have in your face. Yes, there you can straightaway see what a meritorious businessman is. I have indeed not often had the honour of transacting so-called great matters with Mr Zacharias Boldt, for Mr Zacharias is a cautious and scrupulous man. But why? I am not begrudging you it. Truthfully to God, I begrudge you it so little, Mr Zacharias Boldt, that I bring both a great joy and a great business to your house today. Why do you look at me so? It is true, as true as I stand here. Is this my right hand? That it is, Mr Boldt. Now then, in my hand I carry the great joy. And is this not perhaps my left? Now see, in this hand I hold the great business. You need merely take hold, Mr Boldt, of both at once, and you will later say after me, 'there old honest Katz brought something to my house', — — now what great thing shall I profess to you? — Superb, superb, A1."

After this address, Mr Katz bent far back, pushed his body forward a little, and looked at his opposite inquiringly for what impression his words of temptation could have left behind perhaps on this creased leathery countenance. But the effort was wasted; Zacharias Boldt remained motionless like a stout sphinx. He continued counting his cobblestones indifferently, to finally bring out as if without reason and completely disinterestedly, "Do you perhaps want to buy a horse from me? Beautiful, I have two. Then come in to the stables."

The little dealer in the yellow coat floundered back and forth a little, and seemed to get into a greater excitement.

"Buying?", he called in answer. "Now of course I want to buy from you. I want to buy a lot from you, and I want to pay you a lot, as true as I live. But you have something else though, Mr Zacharias Boldt, in your house other than mere four-legged animals. I tell you, you have two-legged creatures with which you could make an impression at the wedding of the Crown Princess. You know already what I mean!"

"No," the horse dealer said morosely, "I don't know."

"God save us," Daniel Katz cried excitedly opposite this lack of comprehension, and raised his hands up fending or pointing. "The man has a jewel of a daughter, what am I saying, an entire diamond necklace, and pretends not to know. Mr Zacharias Boldt, what is your entire stud farm all together against the quite unique breed which you have started in your loving marital home. And see — I take it as a good sign — there stands your daughter Miss Louise right before the stables and feeding the chickens. Now, what shall I say? She is a picture, so lovely that the tears rise in the eyes of an old man like me. How lusty and well-nourished one looks when Miss Louise stoops her curved and noble limbs. A delight. What a relaxation exists in her charms, and how pliantly her joints move. A genuine, Arab stallion, truthfully to God, could belong to the Sultan himself, could not be in a better condition."

At this point, Daniel Katz moved his head dreamily, and heatedly pushed his top hat a little from his forehead, before he continued, "God, what a smashing impression such a capital piece must make on a well situated young man. And as we are just speaking, Mr Zacharias Boldt, I carry this aforesaid young man in my right hand. He is, if you want to know his name — —".

No, this fat stable owner though really possessed a hardened disposition. For without paying the slightest attention to the mysterious intimations of his business associate, he strode wide-legged and with his rocking gait to the stable doors, which he pushed open with a rough kick. Then he waved to the dealer energetically with his lumpish head, "Well, now come on."

"A very strange gentleman," Daniel Katz thought. "How can you make a wide-ranging business with such a wild man? A difficult undertaking in fact," he added as he rubbed the hair on his temples worriedly, "now, we will see."

Amidst these thoughts, Mr Katz strolled in.

See there, the stables were exemplarily kept. Everywhere you saw fresh straw heaped, from the mangers a strongly scented hay thrust forth, and in the wooden partitions stood three horses, cleanly curried and brushed. They were groaning loudly with contentment as they fed snuffling and chewing on the golden yellow oats from the manger. Hey, how the ears of both the well-nourished browns pricked up when the visitors entered. Only the white mare in the last stall gave no sign of recognition. She just airily moved her long cascading, silky tail, and otherwise stood motionless. And the owner seemed to want to steer the attention of his guest directly away from this white mare. At least, he placed himself directly before her stall so that he blocked Mr Daniel Katz's view, and threw out curtly and spitting, "Beautiful animals, the two browns."

"Well, yes, they are beautiful," Mr Daniel Katz replied, although he endeavoured inconspicuously to let his gaze wander over the third stall.

"Plough horses and wagon horses," Zacharias Boldt explained with praise. "And healthy — fighting fit."

"Beautiful, but —".

"Are you finding perhaps a problem?" the stable master growled. "I would very much refuse to tolerate it, I am an honest man."

"God, why the uncouthness?", Mr Daniel Katz parried. "Have I said a wrong word? How would I forget so much my respect, and talk of problems in the presence of these tidy animals?"

With these words, he tapped one of the browns lightly on the back without especial joy. And the gaze of the little yellow squire meanwhile drilled more and more avidly across to the third stall which was eluding him so insistently.

"But why are you saying nothing at all about the white mare? She gleams like white silver which has been polished!"

"Leave it," Zacharias Boldt parried irritably, and made a dismissive gesture.

"Why?"

"Well, why. I am an honest man, the nag is nothing to a connoisseur. Don't you see, Mr Daniel Katz, that I have painted the animal from top to bottom?"

"No, not a trace," the horse dealer protested, and he really saw nothing. The steed's coat gleamed and shimmered like metal. "It is a glorious item though," he continued.

"But it has a hare's hock, and is lame," the stable owner contradicted grumpily. "Now stop there, I am not selling the animal to you."

"What?" the visitor lamented in rising fury. "Do you consider me to really be so lacking in knowledge that I should believe all that? The animal does not have a hare's hock, and it's not lame. And it is not painted. Not a trace. From where would you have possessed such a trick, Mr Zacharias, of which I have not heard anything yet in all my days? I want to buy precisely this animal from you, for amongst us, it will be something quite special just because you don't want to give it to me. And I will offer you 500 marks for it. All of 500 marks, not including the great joy which I will yet bring you in addition."

"600," the owner growled, and struck his hand against the wood. "Not a pfennig less."

And amidst endless cursing and negotiating, amidst eternal bristling of the seller, and just as unrelenting covetousness of the purchaser, the sale was finally concluded.

"Well okay," Zacharias Boldt cried in fullest fury, "I want nothing more to do with the whole story. Fixed."

And Mr Daniel Katz sighed "fixed" exceedingly relieved after him, whereby he wiped the sweat from his forehead with his red handkerchief.

"And now, Mr Zacharias, let us not forget the quite great joy. Why should I not approach you businesslike? So quite short and quite sweet. The son of the taverner Gülzow in Wolgast, who has the beautiful place of relaxation, you know already, loves your daughter Miss Louise. What is meant by loves? He has it straight with the desire. And the father has two mortgages of 30,000 marks on my own house in Knopfstraße. Should I tell you yet more of the sophistication of this family? And the only condition is, the wedding must be in fourteen days, for the head barmaid has become ill, and the young woman shall hence look a bit to her rights. What do you say to this fortune, Mr Boldt?"

But remarkably, this so enormously advantageous offering did not seem at all even to be evident to the father. He grudgingly spat again onto his boot, and shook his entire body in vigorous aversion, until he finally erupted in a rough tone, "Nothing can become of that."

"What, you decline Gülzow's son? You decline the first and second mortgages on my house? Mr Zacharias Boldt, shall I consider you perhaps to be ill?"

"It won't work," the stable owner grumbled somewhat more indignantly. "She has a blemish."

"Who? Your Miss Louise?"

"Yes, a quite large one."

"Such a thing is unprecedented," the dealer fretted. "Does she not look like loveliness itself? Does not her golden red hair sparkle on her head as if an abacus of pure gold coins were up there? I tell you, you are no connoisseur, Mr Boldt."

"But," the father said, as he turned curtly determined towards the door, "there is nothing doing with the girl, for she gives everything away which she has in body and soul."

It was hardly describable what a remarkable leap in the air Mr Daniel Katz accomplished when he had absorbed this main objection of the disinclined father. He actually proceeded over a bale of straw, before he held back his business associate by his thick golden watch chain.

"What a funny man you are," he ascertained quite happily. "The party is fixed anyway. If that is the only blemish of your daughter Miss Louise, then I will announce it today in Gülzow's public bar, and you shall see that tomorrow the suitor will stand before you in a new black suit coat which I will also provide for him, and the entire story will be concluded in an instant. I wish such a blemish on all Christian and all Jewish children. Precisely a golden blemish, Mr Boldt. What does that amount to with the good circumstances of the Gülzows? May she give away for my sake what she has in body and soul."

***

Four weeks passed in the countryside, and then it transpired that "Bismarck" also stood the test glowingly this time.

It was a stormy autumn day. The poplars on both sides of the main road nodded and bowed in the hefty wind, and a short rain-shower dusted the Boldt property.

Then a light carriage rolled up the country road. It stopped before the entrance of the spacious yard, and Mr Daniel Katz sprang down from it in his yellow squire's coat and the seriously rain-damaged top hat. The next moment, the little man headed, vigorously gesticulating, over to his massive business associate who seemed to be lost in an instructive conversation over dog breeding with the old gaunt shepherd Sturm before the stable doors. Mr Zacharias Boldt made not the slightest glance to the new arrival. And yet it was as if a strange, satisfied smile played about his thick lips as soon as noticed the excited man approaching.

"Mr Boldt," the yellow squire cried now without any preliminaries. And after the arrival had announced himself so stormily, the farm owner could not hold off any-more raising his eyes to him.

"Hello, Mr Katz," he began amicably. "And how are things?"

Only, the little man floundered as if a giant fist had drawn him onto a wire and was now taking pleasure in wrenching the arms and legs of this toy.

"What, how should things be?" he expressed his indignation with the last of his moderation. "When one is — how shall I say it — kept in the dark by a dear and trusted business associate!"

Only, he did not get any further. The horse dealer straightened up menacingly, and then balled his fist meaningfully.

"What?", he growled with his hoarse voice, "Do you perhaps want to say here before a witness, namely before the shepherd Mr Sturm, that I have deceived you? With what, if I may ask? I advise you, however, do take care."

"Also take care?", Mr Daniel Katz flailed in response, now losing all the best part of his senses. "Is that perhaps a white horse which after three weeks suddenly looks yellow? Yellow, Mr Boldt," he reinforced distress-fully, "yellow, like a proper lemon from Messina. What shall I do with a yellow, white horse which also has a hare's hock and is lame? The animal truly has jaundice."

"Yes," the farm owner nodded simply and evenly, as the creases in his leathery countenance began to twitch and tremble. "There you are right. Did I not report all that to you in advance in accordance with the truth?"

"Yes, but —", Daniel Katz interrupted imploringly, now having to skip with fury unrelentingly from one leg to the other. "Yes, but I thought —".

"Quiet," the dealer reprimanded him. "And did I not share with you that I had painted the ugly old beast? And today I can add that for the tincture, which I obtained directly from a mariner in Stettin, I paid thirty marks cash. Is that not enough?"

"He said it, he said it," Daniel Katz now cried beside himself. "Has one ever heard the like, that one brings forth such a coarse truth over his own wares? Has a businessman ever believed the one who shoos away? And," he continued as, in his excitement, he dabbed his forehead incessantly with his red handkerchief, "even if I wanted to turn a blind eye to it. How you have swindled me over the other matter. Swindled is not the expression. I assure you, you have destroyed my entire reputation. No, what sort of woman have I recommended to Gülzow for his house? Here, read yourself the letter I received. Truly, it looks as if he is putting the wares at my disposal again after four weeks. Look, here it is. After fourteen days, your daughter Miss Louise had already been encountered with the barman, with her own barman in an intimate discussion. How do you like that, Mr Boldt?"

But the beset father just serenely lowered his industrious hands into his trouser pockets, and confirmed calmly, "Did I not also share that with you. Can you deny that I said she gives everything away which she has in body and soul? Now then, is that not an expression which educated people speak when they converse over such an unspeakable thing? Has Louise perhaps done anything else?"

Daniel Katz stood rigidly. He just opened his mouth from time to time, wide and snapping like a pike which has been drawn onto dry land. You could distinctly read from his reddened countenance that he wanted to rage in fury anew. Only, the admiration for the opponent who was so much superior to him seemed gradually to win the upper hand.

"Mr Boldt, it is a piece of art like I have never experienced before in my practice. But since we will perhaps do business together once more, I want to forgive you the hustling. Certainly only under one condition. You must share with me, on the spot, from whom you have learnt the great art of doing business with the truth. Perhaps I will also learn it, and compensate myself with it for my great losses. Will you?"

"Why not?", the horse dealer grumbled, being very flattered, and turned his thick golden watch chain smugly. "I read in the newspapers once that our great Bismarck invented the truth as a tool of state. With the truth in particular, my dear Katz, he always kept all the other asses in the dark, and they racked their brains for a long time over what the man had meant when he had already had them in his pocket long before. Now look, I have also such a little piece of Bismarck in me, and use it with risky business. And now go home and rejoice over the means. But I tell you straightaway, if you want to perhaps use it on me, I know the jest, I will believe you word for word. And now adieu, and get better."

With that the three men parted.

But when shepherd Sturm was sitting some time later under his hollow willow, and his Karo placed his head on his knee thoughtfully to blink up at him with clever eyes, the old man spoke from the depths of his mind, "Yes, yes, my boy, you surely think too about what you just heard. I tell you it is a dangerous thing with the truth, and quite different to how it is in books. They say in particular that it is a short dark path through which you gradually climb up to the bright light. But I have never found it so, Karo. The truth is rather a long dark cliff path from which you find no way out. The longer you run, the darker it becomes around you. But finally you arrive at a rocky corner, and there stands a radiant white angel with silver wings who looks at you sadly from its bright eyes and says, 'Wanderer, you will not find the end, for no man on earth knows where the truth leads. Whether into the bright heights, or into the depths dark as night. And hence it is good for the human temper if it takes pause at a specific place and sits down.' Look, Karo, and that I have long done, and hence things go well for us."

And when the shepherd had spoken thus, the sun broke out from the rain clouds, and gilded warmly and playfully the leaves of the old willow which had given the meadow shelter from the dampness up to then.

LITTLE FIK

A Wondrous Occurrence from the Bay

Little Fik

It was a winter's day. Heavy and impenetrable, massively balled up as if millions of white doves were plunging to earth wearily and dying in enormous flocks, the massive snowflakes whirled down onto the lonely water meadows.

No sound arose, no noise interrupted this white indifference, nothing seemed to be able to hinder that incessant dying. But across from the firmly frozen path, it sometimes drove the sea to a constant distant moaning. Out there the captive giantess was lamenting under her unbreachable bonds and shackles of ice.

"Just wait — just wait — when I first get my powers back — how I will tear at you, you mob!

And then it groaned again from its clenched chest, "Huh, huh", until the shiny cover of ice seemed to crumble.

On such a dreary day, when the sun had already disappeared behind the white wads, and the easterly was strolling about the snow-buried fishing village loudly whining and grumbling, on such a dozing day, the unfamiliar woman stepped for the first time into the oddly uneven cottage of the tailor Chris Husen. She took a look at the pitch-black floor, over which two heavy beams passed at man height, as if she intended to plunge down any moment, and then the visitor tapped with the heel of her boot gently on the well-worn red bricks of the floor, "A little oil lamp is missing on the wall here," she said with her calm voice as her finger was already indicating the place where the desired thing would be attached. "And then, the floor here must be patched with clay. Otherwise you'll stumble."

Behind her in the darkness, something danced, and after the strangely eccentric, somewhat stooped figure of the tailor Chris Husen, who at this moment was leading over the threshold of his cottage for the second time in his life a wife wedded to him — after the tailor had cleared his throat, giggling oddly, he tapped his spidery finger approvingly on the back of the woman walking in front of him.

God, God, what pretty firm flesh his current one had though. That was something. Yes, that certainly meant something other than the eternal complaining which his late Sophie could offer him during her long illness and in her eternal state of pain. Eh yes, now here a proper woman would be walking around with dark, shiny hair under which such bright grey eyes peered forth; a wife who knew how to rock neatly and properly at the hips. No, the way she did that. Indeed he did not see it rightly in the darkness, but he felt it though. And this consciousness caused him such a joy that the little tailor again fell into his accustomed dance step, and began laughing loudly, "Yes, yes, Marik, dear beautiful Marik", he whispered in her ear, and at the same time, he tried to stroke the erectly waiting woman affectionately on the cheek. "Everything shall be as you want it. For you understand your business. That I note already. And since you can also finish women's clothes, we will become big. In three, four, five years, we will become big. Pay attention, Marik. And now I will open the door here so that you can see the most beautiful thing of all. The great garland about the table, and on the small cupboard, the black kerosene lamp made of porcelain. I did not ever want to buy it for my first wife. But for you, my pretty, sweet, black-haired child, I purchased it straightaway."

He tore open the door, doubled up as if he wanted to make a strange dance-master's bow, and then he pointed with outstretched arm into the small, humble room through whose clouded glass windows the twilight oozed bleakly and spongily. It looked as if dirty, grey cobwebs were drawn through the entire humble space, lurking there only to envelop and embrace incautious intruders.

"And that, dear, good, beautiful Marik, is little Fik."

Remarkably, the tone with which the dancing tailor gave this explanation contained a light air of apology, but at the same time also something so exaggeratedly suggestive, as if Chris Husen had until then in his home been feeding up an absolutely strange fabulous being which he now intended to show for the first time in his menagerie to an esteemed audience.

"Little Fik," he repeated, "yes, yes, little Fik, my sweet Marik. Look, at her 16 years, she is now almost as tall as you. That is, not quite so tall, and also not yet so prettily full and round as you are, my sweet treasure. No, no, she cannot think of that. For anyway, where is to be found such a woman and beauty as you are, my sweetie. So plump and so warm and — and — anyway. Yes, and she is also right lively. Some would say a little wild. But under your still, white and gentle hand, she will soon unlearn all that. And now, little Fik, come forward, and give a little curtsy before your new and future mother. And then give her your hand, and tell her that you will always be fond of her and be right obedient to her."

The two entering remained at the door, and their gazes crossed with that of little Fik.

Yes, there the tall-grown thing stood with her curly, flaming red hair, and her remarkably dark eyes which lay under this red roof like two restless, strange animals; there she stood, and as she rubbed her short stub nose embarrassedly, she tore with the other hand half in fear at her white apron which was slung for the festivity of the rare day over her dark blue, and much too short, little cloth dress. A hasty cough forced itself from between her conspicuously red lips, it seemed, as if she wanted to stammer a greeting, but the quick, fitful breaths were unable to form any audible sound.

Still the other two waited. And a stillness occurred, pressing, paralysing, and yet voluble. Truly, the cobwebs in the humble room had captured a new being.

Suddenly life surged into the misshapen young husband. With a quick look at the motionless countenance of his better half, he skipped behind the table as if he intended now inevitably to seek a partner for the round dance common to those districts, and grasped the small hand of his child, who towered over him by a head.

Little Fik brooded. The two arrivals as well as the great tenderness with which the strange woman was lavished by the sweet dancer seemed openly to bring forth an amusing impression on her temper, a temper which tended so much to exuberance.

No, her father Chris Husen had never before hopped and skipped so strangely and so unbelievingly funnily. And how wondrous he looked when he sought so intimately and insistently to stroke the shoulders and arms of the black-haired young woman with his scrawny fingers, which had taken on entirely the form of enormous darning needles.

Then she twisted her great red mouth to laugh. And under the heaped red roof at the same moment, both the dark wild animals, awoken to life, sprang up. A full look met the stranger. Then the sixteen year old thrust herself suddenly with her boyishly supple limbs from behind the table, headed without any words in advance to the shocked woman, and grasped with wild astonishment at the small bouquet of violets which the bride held in her hand.

"Look," blared forth shrilly and with overly loud giggling from the child's breast, "look — hey — violets. Proper violets. I have never seen such in winter before. Give me one!"

And before the surprised woman could defend herself, or even arrive at a decision, yes, before Chris Husen was even able to give up his stooped dance pose, there — with an irresistible grasp — little Fik had pulled the remarkable blue flowers to herself, had stuffed them in her mouth as if it were a case of consuming a precious morsel, and already her penetrating child's cry was shrilling from the windows onto the village street, "Karl — Karl Heinrich, come out. I have blue flowers. And we will tie them around the neck of your dog Pax. Pretty — pretty."

The next moment, you could hear clattering steps originating from the wooden clogs of the girl storming away, and the married couple found themselves alone.

"Yes," Marik Husen said, as she tried to laugh a little, to the concerned tailor who had sunken in bashfulness onto the green rep sofa behind the oval table, "she is a bit wild, isn't she, Chris?"

"Yes, yes, Marik, but —".

"Leave it, I know that her mother has been gone from her for three years already."

Gone from her? Chris Husen tore his mouth open, he placed his hand on his heart, and the tears entered his slightly agitated bluish green fisheyes. No, how his current wife brought it up! How delicate and well-worded. Certainly, no other person in all of Moorluke could talk like that. So kindhearted, and with such feeling. And as the young woman now moved up close to the back of the sofa so that her arm almost had to touch his cheek, he began again with his loving obtrusiveness to stroke down her slender figure.

Beautiful — beautiful, oh, his fingertips right tingled as if they were stroking back and forth over beautiful satin. Yes, yes, quite right, over beautiful satin destined for the vest lining of a leading fisherman. Yes, his Marik was a glorious creature. Even if she remained a bit quiet and uncommunicative for the time being. But that would find its own way out. The familiarity certainly fitted, when — when —.

With an unexpected movement, Chris Husen drew his wife next to himself on the sofa, and as he slung his arm around the unmoving woman, he whispered in her ear with that giggle which he foolishly tended to always use for important things, "Marik, my sweetie, I know. I see you, and I hear you. You are good. Also towards little Fik. From you, she can learn womanliness, and whatever else behoves. And to show you, my darling, what a great manly trust I embrace towards you, I will place little Fik, my dear daughter, entirely in your beautiful hands. Yes, yes, in your beautiful hands, give me one here."

And with that, Chris Husen attempted actually to lead the slender white hand of the silent woman to his carp's snout according to gentlemanly and chivalrous custom.

He smacked loudly with delight.

"Oh, how white — how white. Yes, yes, Marik, our joy is very great. Are you tired already?"

"No," his wife responded calmly.

The tailor moved back and forth several times. He let his gaze sweep blearily through the humble room to the two abutting alcoves, until he finally began anew, "Shall we drink a glass of wine? I have good Bordeaux which was only recently smuggled in. What do you think?"

The black-haired Marik nodded.

Now Chris Husen was stroking her hesitantly over the knee. The black silk material rustled under his hand. "Shall I, shall I also call for Fik?", he tried to inquire at this opportunity. Only, the young woman considered drawing in the minor obviously to be ill-timed. A child, she decided, while she rose as if unintentionally, does not belong during such things. And as she slowly skimmed past the smaller alcove, she uttered with her black eyelashes deeply lowered, "Who sleeps here?"

"There? Oh, merely little Fik."

"So, and over there?"

At this question, the young husband rose, however, and hopped like a happy wagtail to the woman watching him with astonishment.

"Over there, Marik," he repeated delightedly, "well yes, you see, that is our room. You will see already how quiet and cosy it is. It leads out to our courtyard, and nothing disturbs you there which you don't want to be disturbed by. Do you understand?"

Only, the young woman just shook her head. "Good," she said, "but it is not right."

"What do you mean, my sweet Marik?"

"Well, that the child shall live so close to us here. That must not be. Have you not thought about that surely, Chris?"

"No, no, truly not."

"Now you see," his wife continued, "but up under the roof there is certainly still a loft room, would it not be more proper if from now on little Fik —".

The tailor writhed. "Yes, but this room," he intended to object.

In the meantime, his wife had already returned to the larger alcove. Now she turned, and her black eyelashes rose heavily and slowly. "Well good," she responded as if she had received his word of agreement long before, "then she shall sleep up there from now on. Right, Chris? And now fetch the wine."

Then the tailor jumped, struck by the power of this gaze, whinnied like a horse which has been stung by a bee, and crept to one of the deepest corners of the hall, where his sparkling treasure from Bordeaux lay hidden.

No more was spoken of little Fik on this evening.

***

But the next morning, the dark-haired Marik took the education of little Fik in her hand. In her slender white hand which had acquired something so absolutely supple and graceful from the habit of sewing.

The first lesson, however, proceeded thus.

It was early in the morning. The newly married woman was crouching on a stool between the red brick walls of the kitchen, and as she propped her head in both hands, she listened raptly to the loud singing and bleating of her husband. Separated from her by the eternally dark hallway, he was enthroned in his workplace kneeling on a gleamingly polished wooden board, whereby he blared songs so incoherently and confusedly that their text could only be explained by budding young love:

> Hey, hey — hey, hey,
> In my tailory,
> Here I sit and make music
> For Marik!

And then again:

> Oy, oy — oy, oy,
> How I am full of joy,
> Am yet already grey in life
> And have a young wife!

The sharp notes shrilled through the entire house, and struck the bare walls so that the young wife had to hear some words twice. It seemed to hurt her ears. It twitched about her mouth, and as her sharp grey eyes opened, she moved her finger back and forth restlessly as if she intended to grasp something. At this moment, her gaze fell through the low kitchen window out into the courtyard which was surrounded by an iced-up wooden fence.

What was that? — Slowly the young woman rose, propped herself with both hands on the broad window sill, and stared out into the dreary winter's day.

And it really was a strange picture which was offered to her.

Outside there were snowflakes, nothing but regularly whirling down white down, soundless and inaudible, and in the midst of this floating play, little Fik in her much too short blue duffel skirt, bare-headed, and in wooden clogs. The young woman stepped back, and grasped her forehead for a moment. Was she deceived by the incessant whirling of the snow, or was the outrageous thing she was seeing out there really true? But no, the picture did not change, it remained always the same. There on the white covering of snow, there little Fik was dancing with raised childish legs wildly, and yet at the same time with a gentle swing to those absurd melodies which her father had just then invented on his tailor's table. Sometimes she clattered with her wooden clogs, other times she tossed her leg out again to pull straight after at her skirts as if she were unable to contain herself for joy over this musical enjoyment in the middle of the driving snow.

Her movements became wilder and wilder and ever madder. The tall girl's breath steamed through the white dance, and at the same time, her hair was lit up like a red flame which wanted to rise despite the icy wind and snow.

Hey, hey — hey, hey,

In my tailory —

Her skirt rustled loudly, and her wooden clogs clattered as if they were being pulled with rare energy onto the iced-up cobblestones.

Here I sit and make music
For Marik.

Here the dancer spun around suddenly on one leg as if seized by a whirlwind, and as she stretched her arms up high, she doubtlessly intended just then to make a quite special leap which would certainly have to exceed all the previous ones. Then — then misfortune approached, the white thread of her fate tore crackling, and for a long time, a black one was drawn onto the spool in its place.

Oh woe, oh woe! Little Fik shrieked. With the wild spinning, the wooden clog suddenly flew from her feet, and a second later it clattered hurtling through the pane of the kitchen window, right before the feet of the calm observer.

The shards sprayed about, and through the resulting jagged hole in the window, the eyes of both women sought each other and met.

In extreme embarrassment, little Fik put the fingers of both hands to her mouth. What will the unfamiliar woman do now? Quite certainly, she would have to storm out the next moment, a stick in her hand, in order to chastise the wild girl. Or would she just pull the step-daughter's red hair?

Oh, what sorrow, little Fik already felt the terrible pains quite distinctly which this unaccustomed treatment must cause her. But none of that happened. The black-haired Marik barely moved. But then she waved almost imperceptibly to the fearfully shaking girl with her pretty little white finger.

"Come in, Fik."

Only, the girl waiting outside slowly shook her head. In now? Oh, she knows already that then the chastising would follow inside. Perhaps she will be shut up in the good room with the green rep furniture, and locked away for a morning. Oh no, she is not so stupid.

Half thoughtlessly and half reluctantly, she remained in the courtyard. And it is strange how the cold, which is rising up from the clog-less, little bare foot, compels her to hide it under the protective skirt. Meanwhile in the kitchen, the black-haired Marik has still not changed her gentle facial features. She just stretches her hand out to the resultant hole in the window to once more, and just as calmly, yes, almost dispassionately, command the obdurate or intimidated child to come to her.

"Come, little one," she motioned anew. "I have something to say to you."

Little Fik did not stir.

Then suddenly — without the unfamiliar woman having given up her position or having made any vigorous movement, then —

Why does little Fik start and begin to tremble all over? Dear God, she had never observed such a thing in Moorluke. Is is really possible? No, no, quite certainly, the light grey eyes of the unfamiliar woman have suddenly turned greenish black.

Greenish black, like the toxic pond over there in the ancient grove of gods about which the children were already warned so insistently in school. And these eyes are subduing her, paralysing the will of the little defiant girl, and drawing the child to themselves as if through a dark magical power.

My God, my God, what a fear! Now she must let down the raised foot, straightaway she feels how the icy coldness of the snow penetrates through the woollen stocking, and a few moments later, the girl is creeping, groping timidly along the wall, then through into the eternally dark hallway. Now she stands hesitantly and falteringly on the threshold of the kitchen. A pot hums on the wood-stove, and from above the frightened girl still hears the confused melodies of her father:

> Oy, oy — oy, oy,
> How I am full of joy,
> Am yet already grey in life
> And have a young wife!

That wife, however, to whom all these homages applied, stood erectly in the middle of the red space of the kitchen, and only the playful flames of the stove were able to lend her countenance some liveliness. But her well-proportioned figure nevertheless loomed beautiful and full and slender.

"Now pick up the clog," Marik began, "and put it on, my child."

And as she placed her hand on the bare neck of the daughter, on that place where it arched down to her breast, she continued calmly, "Why must you dance in the morning? Tell me that!"

"Oh, just because," little Fik replied, although it seemed to her for the first time in her life as if the words had turned to stones in her throat.

She swallowed with difficulty, and choked on it.

The slender finger of the black-haired woman buried itself instinctively somewhat deeper into the soft flesh of the girl standing before her so that Fik had to cough heftily against her own intention.

"Quiet", the new mother continued. "You can see what you wreak with such wild behaviour, little Fik. The glazier will certainly be charging a mark for this windowpane. Have you ever earned a mark before?"

"No," little Fik responded defiantly, and something like a secret aversion towards this sort of gentle instruction rose up in her, "that I have not needed to."

"So, so." The stepmother stroked her cheek. "You see, little Fik, we want to get along well with one another, and I am in favour of every person close to me having their work to perform, without grumbling and without opposition, that is understood by itself. And you are already a tall girl, and must you not repay your father, who looks so faithfully after you, for a part of your upkeep through some sort of work? Tell me please, can you sew?"

"Badly," little Fik responded curtly, and with that she thought of the ugly rattling of the large shears in her father's workplace which had seemed to her in earlier days to always be suspicious and unlucky.

"So you can't?", the mother continued. "I will show you this afternoon. And now, can you peel potatoes?"

Just then the little one wanted to say no again in high aversion, when it occurred to her again as if that greenish black spark was beginning to glimmer from the eyes of her oppressor. Almighty, did it not seethe just like the eyes of that strange black snake which had curled up twitching on a branch of the hazelnut tree at the back of the garden the previous summer?

Horrifying!

And all of a sudden, all the folk tales of the evil stepmother passed through the mind of the startled girl. And this scourging memory subdued her power of resistance completely. With a deep sigh, she sank onto the kitchen stool on which Marik had been crouching lost in dreams shortly before, and quietly, and furtively sobbing, she threw both hands over her face.

"What's wrong?", Marik inquired, very astonished.

Truly, this child was becoming more and more incomprehensible to her, and all the patience which she had arduously collected for this difficult lesson began to fall away and escape from her. She wrinkled her brow brusquely.

"Why are you crying?"

"I'm not crying."

"So then!"

The tone of this exclamation trembled slightly. "Then sit here in the corner next to the water butt and peel these potatoes. Make sure it is done."

Quarter of an hour later, you could find the red-haired thing pressed deeply into the corner between the water butt and the wall, and performing with awkward and freezing hands the work she so hated and was forced to do. The water constantly sprayed high when she threw one of the peeled potatoes into the pot standing next to her which Marik had filled with well water before she left the kitchen.

Only, the red-haired wild child could not remain for long at the prescribed activity. The water of the pot splashed up at ever longer intervals, for little Fik sat with neck stretched forward to listen and then brood again. Over there in the workplace of her father it had become still in fact. Vague, disjointed syllables fluttered across to the curious girl, and from time to time, she caught a noise which the girl was hardly able to explain.

How strange! Chris Husen seemed to be caressing his young wife. Yes, he must even be kissing her occasionally, it sounded so smackingly loud and obtrusive.

And now — oh, that was good — now the door to the workplace was also affected by the air pressure of the breeze, and opened a crack. The redhead could now peer across almost unhindered. And as she had painted it in her child's imagination, the expected picture now sprang towards her in reality. On his well-polished board, her father crouched with his legs underneath, and had both arms slung around the neck of the young woman whom he sought to draw down with force, and his blissful cries swirled and bleated loudly and emphatically over to the appalled daughter.

"Oh, you sweet Marik, you beautiful, curvy, cosy wife you, how scared I was for you. Believe me, I cannot endure it here in my old seat without you at all, such a thing of love and faithful yearning, I have never felt. And you, Marik? You, my proud, black-haired child, how is it with you? Will you still bide your time for as long as yesterday? No, you won't injure your dear husband any longer, will you, for otherwise, otherwise, my golden treasure, I must leap into the river here from utter grief. See there, where it discharges into the bay. And Marik, you don't want to be to blame for that, do you?"

And the gaunt, emaciated arms, from which the work smock had been pushed back a little, twitched anew, and began struggling with the woman defending herself vigorously from these caresses.

"Come, my child."

"No, leave it, I don't want to."

"What, you are defending yourself? That is just a jest by you, Marik."

Thus it went back and forth, until the young, strong wife grasped her crouching husband by both shoulders to hold him away from herself with strong hands.

"Chris," she said, "I do not like it when a man interrupts his work."

The tailor whined, "But today is something different, Marik," he attempted to move her, and again he stroked her curved hips lovingly at the same time. "Today you belong to me though, my sweetie, for the first day."

But the listener heard cold and unmoved how her stepmother responded, "Now that's enough, Chris, I do not like and simply will not suffer such foolishness, and if you continue thus, then —"

"What then?"

"So leave off," Marik suddenly cried in wildly storming fury and without thinking. And in a complete rage, she suddenly cast the grotesque figure of her husband with a single shove onto the boards of the large tailor's table so that the wood whimpered and groaned.

"Did you not hear," her voice rang out, hoarse with agitation, "that such things are loathsome to me? Now take note!"

"What, what?", the husband started to flare up, thrust out of all the heavens of love, as something quite unforeseen had happened. With a fast movement, little Fik had in fact leapt up in the kitchen. That over there, no, that over there she must not tolerate. The unfamiliar woman wanted here to mistreat her father, and she herself, little Fik, should be forced to peel dirty potatoes here? And all that on the first day since the unfamiliar woman had entered this usually so cheerful house where previously only dance and song had reigned? That was too much! It abruptly began humming and whirring in the girl's head, as always occurred when a quite especially wild thought circled about her temples, like an enormous bird glistening with every colour which strove to snatch her away into the vast distance with its claws.

Now do it, now do it — now throw, the giant vulture thus blared in her ear, as its beak hacked at her forehead.

Then it happened around the ungovernable girl who had until now lacked a guiding hand. With half-stifled cry she jumped up. Drunk with delight, staggering in the feeling of a long saved, glorious revenge, she gathered a handful of the largest potatoes together and now, now she threw the tubers with accurate hands into the workplace, cheering over her misdeed.

Ha, how that struck! Three, four, five. The hard shots had smashed against the head and hair of the unfamiliar woman one after the other, and what now followed raced and stormed thus as if the seconds were overrunning one another, and chasing themselves like furious, biting hounds.

With a leap, the black-haired Marik was over the threshold of the kitchen.

"Did you throw them?"

"Yes, I did."

"Oh, you — you, you girl. You nasty red toad! Now I will show you!"

Hard as iron with clawing grasp, the long, well-tended fingers of the raging woman nestled around the neck of the child, right at the place where they had rested so coaxingly a short time before. And then — a short turn, a twist, a scream, and something flew dully under the kitchen table like a kicked dog.

"Lie there", a voice hissed, forcing itself to a whisper with supernatural strength, although it made an expression as a result like that which only tends to be known from the hissing fox. "Lie there, and woe to you if you dare forth again! Now pay attention, you hatchling, you will soon see how tame you will become."

The next moment, the foot of the beautiful woman kicked once more hard and quick against the sprawled figure.

***

And little Fik really saw. Her education in fact made massive strides. Without the black-haired Marik being inclined originally to calculated brutality, she became day by day more irritated and embittered by the life in the dim dark tailor's house, but especially as a result of the traffic with her so unlikely husband. Yes, gradually the tormenting idea established itself in her that, for every caress by the man so hated in her soul, she would have revenge on someone in this house.

Did the smitten tailor then not notice at all that she had accepted his courtship only in an hour of fear and hardship? At the time, when she had been abandoned by that devil-may-care sailor on whom she had hung her heart, and who now certainly would be whispering in the Argentinian ports the same foolishness in the ears of the hot-blooded Spanish women as he had once to herself in those short, wonderful hours.

Oh, as soon as she thought of the distant man, it boiled up in her. The inconstant man far away, and she, she, tossed aside like an overused toy, until she had now ended up in this dilapidated tailor's home, on an ash heap as it were. In such hours, she started as if lashed by a whip. And then she avenged herself.

Fik did not understood how to sew. She broke the threads, tossed the clothing to be mended into a corner when she thought herself unobserved, yes, recently she had even broke the hated needles with flagrant malice directly before the eyes of the observer.

Snip, snap, so it was right, that must have infuriated the stepmother.

And for that, Marik avenged herself. With a sort of burrowing wantonness, she then passed her slender, well-tended fingers through the red hair of her charge, and tore and ripped about in it for so long until it seemed almost unbelievable to her that the chastised girl was not crying out in raging pain. Only, she waited for that in vain. For in such moments, the girl bit her teeth into her swelling lips, dug them deep into the soft flesh so that drops of blood ran. But she gave out not a sound. She would rather she remained dead on the spot. Yes, rather lie lifeless on the red tiles of the kitchen, with her wonderfully glorious marmoreal countenance encircled by the red hair like a bloody crown of thorns. Just like it was to be read in the beautiful folk tale of Snow White.

And yet this formed only the beginning. The education of the recalcitrant girl should yet arrive at a further accomplishment.

A nasty, dark hour sank over the tailor's house. An hour, usually specified for its being entwined with wreaths and garlands by kindly little hearth spirits.

On a dreary December day, the young wife crouched weary and battered on the stool behind the stove. It was quite dark in the room. Only the bluish flames of the peat fire twitched between the cracked iron rings, and they illuminated her ghostly pale face for moments. But what the black-haired Marik did not notice in her fear and abandonment consisted of the circumstance that little Fik had crept into the furthest corner of the room, behind the water butt, to gaze from there with wild, and yet well-pleased smile at the hardship of the lonely struggling woman. The two dark animals again leapt forth from under the red heaped roof as if they intended to tear apart exhausted game.

A long time passed thus. You could occasionally hear the hissing of the fire raised by the wind, and discern the quiet crying of the young wife.

Oh, that is good, that is good, little Fik thought, whereby she curled up still tighter in her corner.

Then something skipped over the threshold. With his eccentric figure, the tailor Chris Husen hopped into the kitchen, having sought his young wife already in vain over the entire house, to lapse into his usual bleating exultation here since he had finally found the painfully missed woman. He stretched his gaunt neck forward, and moved his head back and forth goat-like.

"Marik, why are you sitting here in the darkness?"

The woman being addressed did not stir. She furtively balled her fist under her apron.

"I am sitting here", she responded calmly.

"Yes, yes, but why in such darkness where your beautiful face cannot be seen? Oh, Marik, I think constantly of your lovely face. It is now as pale as the purest white silk which I may only use for the very best lining. But look, Marik, this time I bring you something! Something which will clothe you quite excellently and will let your slender, proud figure emerge still more. Look, from this grey cloth, I have cut out for you a woolen dress, quite close fitting. And now come, my dear child so that I can fit it on you."

With both hands, the enthused man stretched a grey scrap out to her, and let it flounce up and down before her eyes as if it the gift were actually a jumping jack which would demonstrate his arts.

"I don't like it", Marik countered at this moment, as she again let her head fall.

The tailor was startled then.

"But for God's sake, what is it with you, my dear?" he danced about her, as he sought to grasp the hand of the averted woman.

But as if shuddering from something cold and sticky, she deprived him of what he desired.

"Chris," she murmured, unsettled, "I want to tell you something, I am in a very miserable mood, for — for —".

And then she bent forward and whispered something which was only meant for her husband.

Did it mean something joyful? Did it contain something calamitous? Who could determine that! For while Chris Husen suddenly set off into the wildest springing to and fro after an initial paralysis, whistled and ranted as if his wife had gifted him an intoxicating drink; while the tailor carried on all this fooling about, the black-haired Marik sobbed in fullest, deathliest lament, and pressed her hands to her heart as if she wanted to tear out that double-edged, boring knife from there. But suddenly she faltered. Why did her look have to trail off as if confused and dazzled back there into that corner? What was that strangely glittering little flame licking out there behind the water butt?

Was that not —?

No, no, that was not possible. It seemed impossible, completely unthinkable to her that that hated creature should now also become a witness to her last, most burning humiliation — God! That was too crazy though. It was certainly just a product of her convulsing fever.

Only, the red gleam licked unchanged from out of that mysterious corner.

Then life flared up in the struggling woman. With a single leap, she went to the dreaded place, and grasped. Once, twice, then she had seized both shoulders. The child cried out loudly. This time she really screamed; for she noticed immediately that it could come down in this moment to a struggle for life and death. What she had heard just now swirled only indistinctly through her memory. She lustfully felt at most the one thing, that the hated unfamiliar woman was succumbing under a nameless burden and torment. And she exulted over that, and no sympathy penetrated into her soul, for her education had actually been led by the severity and stress of her instructress as far as a certain perfection.

But now, now she felt faint. All the defiance fluttered away from the girl, for she found herself pulled up again — jerked up by cutting fingers — chest to chest with a maddened enemy.

Paralysed with fright, incapable of any movement, Chris Husen leant with open mouth in his corner. He perceived twitching only how his wife tore down a hazel stick which had hung on the wall until then, and the next moment, the tailor awaited with aching shudders how the hard wood must whistle and descend weightily onto the head of his child.

Blood would flow, yes, red blood! God, help, oh great God, help! But strangely, when he opened his eyes again, nothing had happened there. With wheezing breath, both women stood eye to eye opposite each other, and now he saw with horror how Marik, deathly pale, had let the weapon fall from her hand to emit in supernatural self-control the words, "Go, go to your room — we will yet speak to each other."

Then she stretched her arm imperiously towards the door, and the frightened man perceived still how his child walked across the threshold of the room shuddering and swaying.

***

Little Fik had nestled quite deeply in the pillows of her blue and white checked bed. At base, you could actually call it more of a hiding-away, for the overly short bed covers had been drawn up by the girl high over her head, and all her limbs, which still remained in boyish immaturity, trembled and flew with a chill, tormented by the stabbing cold.

Dear heaven, what sort of a bedroom is meant by this? A barely two steps wide, miserable wooden cranny from whose crude rough walls wooden splinters the length of an arm had detached to now stare into the bare space menacingly. From the diagonal roof beam which passed right over the head of the recumbent girl, an icy drop trickled down from time to time, and fell slapping onto the bed. It could also happen that an entire cloud of dusty snow would waft through the gaps in the roof.

Here little Fik lay, and awaited amidst shivering and gnawing despair the arrival of the unfamiliar woman. Oh, the inexperienced creature felt ever anew with horror how the fearful superiority of her enemy grew as a result of that incomprehensible calm and taciturnity; an enchanting power by which the defenceless child thought herself entwined by constricting cords. Thus she lay, and pondered and pondered.

What could the black-haired Marik wish to share with her now? And why in all the world might the woman have been sobbing in the afternoon in such a heartrending manner? All these thoughts passed through her head, humming and whirring, and then she twitched anew, almost spasmodically, as soon as such an ice-cold drip met her defencelessly exposed shoulder.

And now? Were not steps creaking there on the stairs? They slowly climbed up. Step by step. Little Fik was able to count every single one, since she had leant far out from her pillows. Now the visitor must already be standing before the door. At this moment, an earth-shattering horror penetrated the excited, passionately shaken creature.

No, no, not remaining lying outstretched, not defenceless here in bed! Who could guess? Who was capable of determining whether the intruder would not slowly stride to the bed, and press her fine, supple fingers on the neck of the resting girl for as long as it took until the last breath had escaped, and a still, waxen pale being would have to dream the eternal sleep on the blue and white checked pillows?

That wild idea arose with such clarity before her in this excited minute that she already felt the cold corpse lying right next to her in the bed.

Out — away — far away from here! With both legs, the mindless girl went from her bed, and now stood in her innocent white shirt swaying and shaking opposite the mother entering the room.

"What shall this mean?", Marik asked, completely knocked off balance by the strangeness of the image which was offered to her.

"I — I — I want to go away!"

"Away? Lie down again at once and listen to what I have to say to you. It will not take long."

"But I don't want to — I can't —", the fearfully shaking girl stuttered as a thousand distorted faces arose before her.

Then Marik stepped up to her.

"You are staying", she commanded with her accustomed calm, and grasped the child's arm firmly. With a strong movement, she led her daughter over to the abandoned bed. At this moment, however, little Fik let out a penetrating cry. Right before her, pressed motionless and waxen into the pillows, she saw once more her own lifeless shell lying before herself. And the dead girl had opened her dark eyes, and was staring at her. Then the tormented girl again let out that incomprehensibly animal-like groan, and then — then she had torn herself away. She heard the steps creaking under her bare feet. The next moment, she felt the dull cold of the hallway's stone floor. Already the front door was rattling, and now — a breeze. Oh, what a shiver, now she is taken into the icy arms of the raven-black night.

Calm, wonderful calm begins to caress the expelled girl. A diamond clear starry sky glitters right above her. Individual glowing golden sparks sinks onto her breast and eyes. The strong easterly strides sympathetically up to her and breathes on her.

"Oh, that is warm," little Fik murmured, "that is really very warm."

Then she leans her red head on the ragged chest of the man, and her mind goes to rest.

***

"No, how strange", little Fik thought as she leant out in measureless astonishment from the enormous bed to look around with wide-open eyes in the wondrous room so unfamiliar to her. She grasped her head. Did she suddenly find herself in a narrow, brown paneled cabin? Or was she floating perhaps on distant seas, far away from her home town?

She let her gaze skim about uncomprehendingly. Everywhere dark-brown, oak furniture which had been screwed to the walls as if the owner feared that they could be thrown about by a vigorous swell. And yet it was situated on land. For through a low-placed round cabin window, you could distinctly gaze out on the deathly still, white glistening water meadows which stretched about the bay in impenetrable silence. In a quandary, the redhead shut her eyes again. What a deep silence spread itself in this cabin-like space, and what strange and peculiar objects were scattered everywhere in the peaceful room, without rule as it were. There in a corner was a tall hall clock, fashioned entirely out of round glass columns. Only the clock face at the head consisted of a reddish stone from which the number protruded in enchased gold. Little Fik had never seen the like in her short existence. And then again, the cute imagery on their heads. There behind her bed, so that she could comfortably reach it with her hand, stood a massive brown wooden chest. Certainly, it must not perhaps be assumed that here was an empty, indifferent surface. Oh no, it was much more cheerful around little Fik. From the paneling in particular, a numerous crowd of apes danced forth. Yes, yes, really quite funny little apes, and they were holding onto each other's paws, forming natural chains and wreathes, and stretching their tongues out unembarrassedly to the watcher.

And over this mad bustle, the girl had to laugh out so brightly and loudly that a part of her memory streamed back all of a sudden and as if with hidden magic.

Wait though — wait though — just how had it been?

Trickling, paralysing cold began climbing abruptly to her so beautifully warmed-through limbs. With a blow, the escaped images chased past her awakened mind. There she saw herself in a short little shirt on the raven-black village street, how she crept trembling and shaking behind the bare shrubs by the fence of the tailor's house. And then the enormous flickering starry heaven had slowly sunken down to her. With stiff hands, she had grasped at the glittering balls to warm herself until finally a giant white snowman came striding up to her almost soundlessly to carry her humming and coughing away from there.

A white snowman?

Dear, kind heaven, where was she actually? This dreamy happiness could not last for long! And as she now surveyed her surroundings once more with her timid gaze, it seemed to her as if there were a knocking, shyly, but then more and more distinctly and insistently, on the thick glass of the low round cabin window.

She started in surprise.

No, no doubt existed anymore. Out there before the window, the frozen blue countenance of her father Chris Husen appeared, and now it seemed that the tailor had even succeeded in opening the window a little so that he could whisper through to his daughter.

"Little Fik!"

"No, no, I don't want to!"

"Little Fik, how I have searched for you! Mercy of God, do you know where you are here? Girl, how could you merely stay the night away, and give your dear parents so much of a fright? And for all the world, how can you just sleep here in this bed? Do you not know then who it belongs to?"

"No, who then?", little Fik inquired avidly.

"Lord, Lord!"

The tailor went into his pocket, brought out his eye-catchingly red piece of sackcloth, and began despite the cold to wipe away with ridiculous effort the sweat from his brow. The terrible arrival place of his child seemed to agitate him so heftily.

"Little Fik," he whimpered anew, as he scratched about insecurely at the glass, "do you know who this house belongs to? It belongs to the old mad Captain Witthuhn".

"What?", little Fik cried. And in the first shock of the surprise, she jumped out of bed, and now crouched shivering and shuddering on the hard chest. "Is that not the old man who they call the bat?"

"Of course, of course. What does it matter?", Chris Husen whimpered through the crack in the window. "Bat or even just mouse, because he is never ever seen during the day, and only wakes in the night and goes for a walk. And then, he is also meant to have sworn off speaking. And up here, Fik, in the top room," — here Chris Husen pointed with his wizened fingers to his forehead — "here it is absolutely not ordered right with him. For as much as I know, my daughter, he goes to sea on specific days of the year, naturally around midnight, and in the moonlight, and then, Fik, oh you can believe me, then he throws three large funeral wreaths into the water, and lets them float away, and cries and sobs like a child at the same time. And then, it is not known at all who orders his house! For nobody has seen anyone in here with him. And it only starts smoking from the chimney at nighttime. And does my daughter want to reside with such an old heathen, with such an uncanny fellow? Little Fik, I beg you, I beg you from the depths of my heart, get up straightaway, and come back to me and your good mother. She is certainly and truly sorry for all she has done."

But Chris Husen should not have mentioned that one. For to the bizarre mind of the redhead, it seemed at least much more pleasant to live in the enchanted cabin of old Muhs than it was to return again so quickly and abruptly to the custody of the black-haired Marik. In fact, hardly had she thought this than she drew her white feet again under the massive covers, and hid herself so adroitly under the pillows that the tiny tailor was unable to see her anymore. And in open scorn, she called to him through the narrow crack in the window, "If it means so much to you, then come in, and fetch me!"

"No, no, Fik, that won't work, that you cannot ask for", the tailor shook, and attempted to spring up by the window in comical leaps. "That I mustn't, see, it doesn't really work!"

And the listener heard how her progenitor mixed begging and cursing in a turbid, colourful confusion to finally conclude that he would fetch the black-haired Marik to the window to support him.

"Yes, fetch her," little Fik thought with a grim pleasure. "But if it goes that far, just take care, then I will call old Muhs, and then you will throw your legs about when the bat looks out the window."

And she nestled cosily and comfortably again in the enormous, red-checked bed which lay soft and warming over her like brown sun-filled sheaves at autumn.

***

As twilight crept through the window, little Fik awoke. No hand had offered her food and drink in the meantime, no foot had crossed the threshold evidently, and nothing seemed to have stirred in the empty house. Always the same impenetrable melancholy atmosphere. Little Fik had risen a long time before, and after she had sat timidly on the hard bedstead, she gazed dreamily and at the same time lost about the narrow, brown wooden space.

Outside, sharp icy needles stormed from the sea against the little, low cabin window. And little Fik was freezing. For now the thought first fell heavily on her heart that she possessed no clothing other than her white shirt. But nevertheless, she patiently clasped her hands in her lap, and waited.

For what?

Yes, dear heaven, that she did not know. Solitary and alone, she possessed the folk-tale-like sensation that she must not leave this enchanted home in which the old, unsociable bat nested, he who was only accustomed to undertaking his shadowy excursions at nighttime.

Yes, now she guessed nevertheless at what she was waiting for. In her defiant child's disposition, the ungovernable resolve had established itself simply that she would see and speak to the old eccentric who had withdrawn from all life, yes, it was completely clear to her that he must even have granted to her furthermore his protection against her own who loved her so much.

Her thoughts strayed further and further. Whether the tailor Chris Husen was now already standing with his wife before the small cabin window, and sitting in wait for her?

She rubbed her hands with satisfaction. Might they just; she, little Fik, would not stir here from her place, and even if she had to sit and crouch here into the night.

And again that dark, brooding silence arose before her. It became darker and darker, and in the unheated room, the cold stabbed at her as though with pointed needles.

No, she did not want to endure it any longer. With a quick decision, she ran with her bare feet to the small remarkable chest in the corner from whose slanting top, when it was still light, a wondrous cover embroidered with thick gold had sparkled. Little Fik did not surmise that it was a rare asiatic altarpiece whose embroidery she now slung with a firm grip about her neck to then settle down again in calm waiting on her bedstead. The hours strode past her again. And the hours poured from black jugs an ever denser darkness around her.

The lonely girl heard the village bells tolling the hour quite distantly.

Nine!

Then — oh, praise God, praise God, and yet what a shock at the same time, a noise arose for the first time in the enchanted house. It was as if there were striding with rough boots back and forth on the floor above. Then the listener heard something crack as if pieces of wood were collapsing in a woodpile, and straight afterwards, the cheerful sounds of a crackling fire rustled through the house.

Puff, puff, so it went above. Certainly, the sharp wind must blow a just-lit fire cheerily. Now there was a rattling as if crockery were being fetched from a cupboard, and straight afterwards, the stairs creaked for the first time under a human step.

It descended lower and lower, and the approaching man seemed to move down ever slower and heavier.

Little Fik waited in her impenetrable darkness, held her breath, and her heart beat so loudly that she thought she could hear it through her chest.

And now, now after such a long time, a light fell through the crack in the door for the first time. It was unlatched from outside, and in the shimmer of a mis-shapen tallow candle which he held away from himself, almost over his head, there stood old Muhs.

The girl bent her head forward. The view which offered itself to her so surprisingly robbed her suddenly of every trace of fear and self-consciousness. For see there, it is not an old wizard with billowing white beard and enormous snowy mane appearing before her out on the threshold, no, the man whom she saw this moment with such sharp grey eyes, he was a tall, rough fifty year old in a beautiful dark blue captain's jacket of fine cloth, broad-shouldered and with lightly greying, blond hair on his head and beard. But his bristly eyebrows sprang forth remarkably snow-white and thick under his tanned forehead.

Old Muhs remained motionless awhile, and seemed to be surprised. But then he hummed something, and after he had shaken his head once more disapprovingly at the presence of the girl, he extended a large brown bowl towards the surprised girl without a word or any preamble. Light steam climbed from the bowl and curled evaporating in the reflection of the light. Everything happened as if a stray dog were being fed by a reluctant hand. But little Fik did not sense that. The strong hunger which governed her made her forget everything. The colourful cloth which she had slung around her, the bare feet which peered out from under the colourful train, yes, even the strange way with which she had infiltrated here. Without hesitation she sprang up to take the brown pot from the bat.

"Oh, thank you — thank you", she murmured at the same time to herself.

In answer, the old Captain shook his head again, and as he measured his guest once more from head to toe, a few words again poured forth from under his dense, un-tended walrus moustache, words which did not imply minor disapproval. Straight afterwards, however, the massive figure turned on its heel with a curt decisive-ness, yes, even as if seized by a sort of fear, to rumble up the steps again without further ado. The steps creaked powerfully. They seemed to have to carry a mighty load.

Little Fik, however, did not think any further about what she had just experienced. If she had been treated like a small stray animal, well good, her gnawing hunger drove her now to tolerate such. She devoured the proffered food ravenously. It was soup with a piece of meat in it. It did not taste good, and spoon as well as knife and fork were missing completely. And yet the meal was devoured in a few minutes. But at this moment, heavy doubt arose for the sated girl. Could she really remain any longer in this unfamiliar house whose owner had not once considered it necessary to ask after her name and status? It occurred to her quite clearly that old Muhs had picked her up half frozen out of the snow on his nocturnal wanderings, and carried her to his home, and that her rescuer, however, now certainly expected his charge would not misuse his hospitality any longer.

What now? Should she really return again to the home of her father where the black-haired Marik certainly waited for her with her silent fury? Never ever. And the fear of the tailor's home gripped her anew, so strongly that the redhead, who had indulged without learning all her compulsive wishes up to then, pulled the colourful cloth closer together about herself with a hefty movement, and opened the door with flying hand. In quick resolve, with a few large steps, and yet inaudibly, because she was running in bare feet, she sprang up the dark stairs. Only a narrow light from above led her. Yes, certainly there in the room above her where she had heard him before so loud and raucous in his actions, there old Muhs must also be found now.

It was something, an unrealised power in her, almost something like the duty of gratitude, which drove her to seek once more the countenance of the man who had provided for her this one beautiful, quiet, peaceful day of rest. Now she stood before the wooden door, and without knocking, she opened it, and stepped inside.

***

Old Muhs sprang surprised from an ancient armchair onto both feet. The wide room was lacking any illumination. No lamps were burning in it, but the cheerful wood-fire which hissed on a half-covered stove threw twitching red light through the dark space, and made it appear for moments to be bright and cosy. The Captain stared in astonishment at the intruding child who hesitated in her colourful oriental garb and bare feet before him. Straight after, however, he shook his head dismissively again, and, from his humming, it sounded almost like a human salutation, "What is it?"

Then little Fik stretched both her hands forward.

"Oh, old Muhs," she began, "I wanted merely to tell you —".

"What?"

"Why I don't want to leave here, and why I cannot go home. Oh, old Muhs, there they want to kill me, and I am so afraid!"

With these words, little Fik was again shaken by such a horror that she plunged at her host without thinking, to clasp both his hands trembling and shaking.

But the old man tore his fingers away gruffly.

"No," he dissented. But then he added, growling between his teeth, "Sit."

With his foot, he pushed a low wooden stool over to her, and after little Fik had sat down in suppressed awe on this seat, she again placed her hands trustingly on the knee of the man who crouched opposite her in his massive armchair, leaning far forward.

And now she wanted to begin her little life story.

But the old man dissented once more. "No," he grunted irritably, "first the pipe."

He struck a match on his vest, and, after he had puffed out a few massive draws from his short mariner's pipe so that little Fik had to cough quietly, which again earned her a cutting glance from the old man, he then demanded, as he clawed at his short beard, "Now sail away."

Little Fik told her story.

And the wild little thing possessed such a remarkably strong gift of imagination that all her words sprang up and came alive. As if the figures which her imagination called forth strode reddish and dazzlingly illuminated by the flames of the stove fire through the room. It was the first time in many years that a human being had been permitted to recite an incident for the old, embittered, and disturbed man in such a comprehensive address. And without him noticing, the lonely man was seized and caught by the life pressing stormily forward. He had long since let his clay pipe fall, and when little Fik now reported her last adventure, how the black-haired Marik had intruded into the girl's miserable bedroom, and how the undressed girl had then been driven out onto the icy village street, old Muhs began repeating words emphasised prominently by the storyteller.

"Black-haired Marik", he murmured, "Chris Husen — ugh, the devil — deep in snow."

And when the little girl had long since finished, the powerful mariner still sat there completely rapt in himself, had both hands placed before his bearded countenance, his wide-open eyes stared through his fingers into the illuminated darkness, and it sounded almost like a groan as he now murmured half lost to himself, "A child — a little child — driven voluntarily to death — people, people — how can they just do that — ugh, the devil!"

And before the girl could recover from her fearful astonishment, old Muhs rose suddenly, and strode with ringing steps to the nearest wall to take down from there a black wooden board. Wordlessly he pushed it into the girl's hand. Then the giant figure threw a few pieces of spruce into the wood-stove, and in the cheerfully crackling light, little Fik could let her gaze sweep over the board presented to her. There three names stood written one under the other with white chalk. Each separated from the other by a large white cross.

Thus recorded there though was "Mother", then a cross, and then likewise "Karl" and "Peter". And again underneath, "Christmas 1898 near the tip of Sumatra".

But little Fik understood.

"God gift them eternal peace", she whispered barely audibly, and wanted to offer the memorial back to the man. But at the same moment, a shrill, uncanny laughter rang in her ear. With a rough, hefty movement, the old man had torn the board from her, and as he now struck the wood with both feet so that it echoed dully in the wide room, he cried in-between with his hoarse voice, "God? — No, no, my daughter, not that name anymore! Since that Christmas, we have both had nothing more to do with each other. He does not come to me, and I don't go to him. And that is good for both of us. And now quiet!"

Then the giant hung the board clattering in its place, and stamped his feet several more times as if in fury, so that everything in the room rattled and trembled.

"People are terrible," he cried at the same time, "they chase the poor and helpless into the deep snow. The rogues do that. But they are simply following in his image, for he acts no differently towards us. And it is all lies and nonsense."

And as little Fik, struck by the vehemence of these words which she barely understood, rose trembling and shivering, she perceived yet how the powerful man paced out the room with wide, heavy steps, his hands behind his back, murmuring to himself ever anew, and with his eyes directed rigidly at the floor where the reflection of the stove fire had formed reddish pools. Suddenly, however, the restless man paused before a massive cupboard. Once more his hand hesitated as if it could not decide to turn the key, but then old Muhs seemed to have mastered himself, for with a sudden jerk, he threw the door back, hesitated once more, and then reached with his massive fist into the opening. A heavy, musty haze, like long stored clothes give off, streamed forth from the old cabinet.

"Here", the Captain murmured, as he threw a pair of shapeless clothes at the surprised child. "May fit. Now they will come alive again. But go quick, I don't want to see them."

With that he slammed the cupboard door shut again with a bang, and an inner voice said to little Fik that it would be high time the old man was left to his solitude again. She just stammered out a "thank you", then she pressed the brown garment to her breast, and crept out the door on her cold feet.

Old Muhs had not turned his head to her. He was doubled up in his armchair, broken down, only now and then did it fall incoherently from his twitching lips, "No, no, we are finished with one another, quite finished. The poor helpless ones in the snow, and the young and strong in the deep water. There is no plan or order. There is nothing anybody can tell me."

And yet the eternal had strewn a symbol of his infinitely gracious power quite close before the despairing man. The stove fire contended with the surrounding darkness, and the light brightened the desolate room, laughing and cheerful.

***

"No", little Fik thought on the next evening, after no sound had arisen again in the slumbering house like the previous day until the late afternoon. "No", she asked herself, "should the old man perhaps lie down and snore again so like a heathen until it is dark, and only come to life in the night? Such a bewitched carry-on could not be at all easy for the man."

And since she was already accustomed to her enormously exhilarating thoughts of lingering under his protection for a quite long stretch of time in this strange home avoided by all other men, the girl decided thus to dissuade the Captain from this stupidity as she called it.

The church bells had already announced the seventh hour.

The child had thus to hurry. She hastily dressed herself in the ridiculously long brown garment which old Muhs had gifted her the previous night, and had to break out into laughter herself at the style of the antiquated, woman's jacket, which fluttered far too wide and ruffled about the neck and bust. Only, it did no harm. A thin cord quickly picked up, as they lay about in hundreds in the corner of her cabin, the dress adroitly belted with it, and now she was ready. A few minutes later, she already stood again in the dark room in which she had spoken with the unsociable man the previous evening.

She held her breath, and cleared her throat.

"Old Muhs", she whispered timidly, "are you there?"

No answer. The unlived-in room lay dark and comfortless before her. Then it became clear to her that the inhabitant of this place must reside elsewhere.

And rightly, a distinct noise penetrated from the adjoining room. Old Muhs was snoring as if a knotted oak trunk was being cut up with an uneven saw, or as if enormous beach boulders were being tossed by a giant fist into the deep sea.

"Ugh", little Fik thought scornfully, as she snapped her fingers, "that is very ugly of him, he must break that habit."

Then she scurried to the covered stove, found a lighter, and lit a candle stump.

She looked around.

Oh, it looked actually really comfortless in this wide unlived-in room. Here utterly black thoughts must creep up on the inhabitant, here they must dance about him to spring finally screaming at his chest and head.

"How would it be", little Fik thought, "if you made this unfriendly space quite bright once more so that the light penetrated into the furthest corners, yes, so that even the high ceiling which you cannot even see could be overrun. Enough wood was present. It lay piled up in long resinous pieces behind the stove.

This idea was so attractive that the redhead could not resist it any longer. The next moment, a number of pieces of wood already lay on the stove, all artfully built up around the candle which little Fik had cleverly placed in the middle.

Hey, that must crackle!

And crackle it really did.

How it puffed, jerked, and cracked. As if blood-red wallpaper made from gleaming French silk had rolled down the whitewashed walls. Thus was the effect on the previously desolate space after only a minute. Even the three white crosses on the black board sprang up in the glow, and danced back and forth solemnly.

Little Fik clapped her hands. But what was that? In a massive bowl which she found next to the stove lay a large end of sausage which her host had certainly set aside for his evening supper that day. Next to it, however, the girl saw a small heap of sweetly scented tea leaves lying there.

"Aha", she determined, "now I know. Now the old man shall learn to his delight how it is done."

Without further timidity, she set two pots of water on the stove and soon had the satisfaction of brightly sparkling bubbles foaming up. "Now the sausage in here", little Fik arranged, "and the tea in the other pot. And look, over there, is that not a kitchen cupboard with plates, knives, and forks? So those utensils are present too. Then old Muhs can finally learn for once how sensible people eat. Right?"

But her actions must have been too noisy. For in the adjoining room, there was suddenly a loud rumbling. A pair of short curses could be heard, then it was as if boots were tossed about, and straight afterwards, a small crack in the door opened, and through it peered the bearded countenance of old Muhs.

"Look," his gruff, hoarse voice grumbled, astonished to the highest degree, and it had no sound of satisfaction in it. "What's happening here, young one?"

"The sausage is ready", little Fik responded unafraid.

"So", her host grouched in response, shaking his head as he pushed his nose a little further through the crack in the door, "did I perhaps instruct you to do that, you strange worm? What is that about? I do not want such a thing! And now let me take a look at the stupid thing".

Clothed in his blue trousers and just a blue woollen shirt, old Muhs hobbled out, and looked down into the sausage pot for a long time and purposefully. But then the tantalisingly emanating aroma seemed nevertheless to take hold of him. Though he seized a plate still grumbling, looked at it from all sides, shaking his head, and after he had placed several pieces of the cooked dish on the porcelain, he drew his shoulders up, and squinted at his guest distrustfully from the side.

"Stupid thing", he said finally between his teeth. And with that he shuffled wordlessly back into his room. It was quite clear that he would also spurn the society of the girl furthermore.

"Oh, he is an old vile ruffian", little Fik grumbled to herself, "and he did not once look at the nice tea."

She poured the aromatic drink into a pair of cups, and then sat down wearily in the large armchair to wait.

She heard clattering from within. Old Muhs must in his seclusion have long since got stuck into the meal of meat.

"No", it went through little Fik's mind, unable to bear it any longer, "the awkward bear must drink something with it. That all cannot be good for him".

Light-footedly, she slipped to the door which had just been so inconsiderately shut before her, and knocked.

Nothing stirred within.

"Old Muhs!", she asked anew.

No answer. Then little Fik banged with balled fist against the wood so that it echoed dully in the wide room.

"Your tea is getting cold, old Muhs", she shouted.

"Well, then let it", it sounded from within, "I did not ask for it."

"Eh, that is an outright sin", the girl knocked anew, enraged.

And when nothing more than an angry grumbling could be heard in the adjoining room, she threw herself back into her chair, outraged, and kicked her feet in fury.

"No, nothing then can be done with him", she decided as the tears of fury entered her dark eyes from outrage, or perhaps also from shame. "Then I will not remain here any longer either. He is no proper Christian at all!"

And then she sat, and stared thoughtlessly into the wonderfully massive flames of the stove.

***

How long she had sat there and dreamt to herself, little Fik later no longer knew anymore. Only, it must have lasted quite a while, for the wood in the stove had burnt down, and the wide room already lay almost veiled in darkness again when little Fik unexpectedly felt her shoulder being touched.

Before her stands old Muhs.

"Pour", he commands as he holds the already emptied teacup to her anew.

So then! Finally his distrust seems overcome. Or has the old Captain's tormenting thirst merely driven him back to the child?

Who knows?

With bright rejoicing, the redhead leaps up from the massive armchair, rushes to the stove, and as she now returns with the filled cup, she is emphatic that old Muhs take his old place in the brown leather chair.

"No", old Muhs parries.

"But yes", the child maintains.

And it is no use to him, he must sit down.

Thus he sits opposite her, for little Fik has moved her low stool right up to his knees, and both now cosily slurp the golden brown drink.

"But it is not right though", the unsociable man judges finally, as he shakes his head discontentedly, "the taste in particular."

"What do you mean, old Muhs?", little Fik inquires, as she taps his knee with her finger, a little aggrieved.

"Vanilla", old Muhs continues, to whom every word is a risk.

"So, that is missing then!"

The old man grumbles. The next moment, however, the girl opens the kitchen cupboard with her accustomed quickness, and now flies back with the desired spice which she tosses in her guardian's cup without further ado.

"Fine", the girl ascertains.

"Well, yes", old Muhs says.

But all of a sudden, he shakes his head in the middle of all the contentment again.

"What now?", the girl inquires, already possessing a certain feel for his needs, as she raises her dark flashing eyes to him.

"Rum", the old man rattles, frowning.

"Yes, so."

And after these spirits are found and poured, old Muhs actually begins to nod his head much more benevolently. Then he even swings his foot back and forth a little.

"Good", he murmurs between his teeth.

"Well yes", little Fik agrees.

The spirits of the sharp drink are already dancing in her mind, and the comforting aroma makes her bolder and bolder. Even old Muhs discovers in himself a burgeoning affinity for being talkative.

"How old?", he inquires, slurping.

Then the redhead confesses to him that her years have arrived in the middle of sixteen and seventeen.

"Hm", the Captain clears his throat, and it is surely only accidental that he lets his sombre eyes sweep for a moment over the nearby board with its crosses for the dead. Only, straight after, he continues, "And what is the woman called?"

And remarkably, little Fik understands him again. "Marik", she declares, "black-haired Marik".

"So, so, write it down for me."

He awkwardly pulls out from his fleece coat a notebook wrapped up several times, like those which widely travelled mariners carry, wets the protruding pencil, and pushes it all into the hands of his guest.

"There, write!"

And after this happens, he raises the girl's countenance by the chin, and bores with his sombre eyes anew into the little history of the child.

"Have you danced before?", he grumbles.

"Yes", little Fik smiles, "I can".

"Well then show!", the old man exhales, as he leans back deeply and comfortably in his chair.

And now a picture sprays up in this dark space which is only dully and for moments seared by red flashes of flames, a picture so young, so lively, so overflowing in love of life and madness, like this desolate room, yes, even the entire snow blown fishing village has hardly ever seen before.

And never, ah never, will the like be seen again.

Little Fik dances.

At first timidly and holding back, conscious of the gaze of her sombre observer, but then fear and shame slide away from her, and the air seethes, scattering the ungovernable, whirling art of this unsettled temper. Pay attention! How the until then so unshapely brown skirt suddenly flutters! The little head is thrown back, the arms intertwine, and as the supple feet assume the most charming poses, the wild thing attempts to make clear and objective to her audience the adventure with the black-haired Marik.

Really and truly, you can hear the clogs clattering, now you see the wooden shoe flying through the splintering window, and now the dancer skips about on one foot as if she were protecting herself from the icy snow.

Oh, how funny it looks!

And then the miracle occurs.

Old Muhs swallows. Once more he attempts to hide his movement behind a cough, but suddenly it breaks out.

He laughs.

Not laughing as you usually hear it, no, an ungovernable thundering, breaking all bonds, as if the sea is breaking its covering of ice and now tossing ice floes against each other. Thus it sounds. And fired up by it, the girl dances more and more wildly, and the man is laughing more and more madly until he suddenly falls silent just as abruptly, and a painful silence occurs.

What is it? The redhead, suddenly rooted to the floor, notices how a thick tear glistens over the cheek of the rising man.

"Go sleep!", the giant figure murmurs then, subdued. And without looking around, old Muhs leaves slowly and shuffling the place of his first delight.

***

Since that experience, little Fik prepared supper for her host every day. She regularly found on parting in the evening a pair of silver coins on the stove, and equipped with these small sums, she wandered the next morning into the village to see to her purchases. On such a walk, it was not uncommon that Chris Husen or the black-haired Marik encountered her. Then the child strode past them both with raised head, and with eyes directed into the distance, and so much defiance and unap-proachability lay then in her features that the tailor as well as his wife gazed after her with open mouth. When the redhead reported such an encounter in the evening to the Captain by the stove fire half anxiously, half gig-gling, and waited with pounding heart for whether it could perhaps occur to her guardian nevertheless to re-turn his guest to that certain misery, old Muhs just creased his forehead scornfully at the mention of these names, to pull out his old notebook straight afterwards, in which he finally inscribed a few new notes.

"Chris Husen", he grumbled in such cases testily to himself, "well wait!"

But usually the two lonely people sat opposite one another, and in the room, illuminated by the friendly flames, a comfortable feeling reigned which increased from evening to evening.

Little Fik had discovered that the old man rejoiced in her artless singing, and since then she had danced and sung for him at the same time. More and more often, she experienced the triumph of old Muhs being hardly able to await the moment of the artistic portrayals. It even frequently happened that he caressed her luscious hair as reward in thanks for her efforts. Then little Fik shook and purred like a besotted kitten.

She had already been resident in the soundless house for over two weeks, and she had already begun thinking about whether it would not be possible to win a life in the light and sun for the Captain too, when a special circumstance occurred in a quite unforeseen way.

One evening — the girl had already been working away busily at the stove for a long time — old Muhs did not appear at the established time. Little Fik wondered; she waited at first patiently, but then she knocked on the door of his bedroom.

Nothing.

The Captain had probably undertaken one of his nocturnal walks, and the child found herself alone. This thought hit her with such forceful violence that she sank in complete incomprehension into the ancient armchair, to then look around the desolate space as if seeking help.

My God, here she found herself entirely alone with the board of the dead there on the wall, on which the crosses wandered up and down ghostily in the reflection of the fire. Her limbs began trembling wildly. Oh, that was bad of old Muhs, that was really bad. And she had become so very accustomed to the company of her old friend that the child became scared for him. In a strange commotion, she threw her hands before her face, and began crying.

"Old Muhs", she sobbed and kicked her foot out at the same time in vehement defiance. "Don't send me away, you are a quite bad old man if you do that."

At this moment, however, cold snowy air wafted to her. Real white flakes swirled towards her in the light of the stove fire to melt quickly on her shivering cheek. With a leap, the girl jumped up. And — oh praise God, praise God — there stood old Muhs before the entrance, and splattered the flakes from his ragged fur.

"Hang it up", he commanded.

She had never followed his orders so quickly before. And when he now sat opposite her again in his accustomed place, she began stroking his knee with both hands in sudden tenderness.

"You're good", she murmured at the same time to herself, "oh, very good!"

But this outbreak of the child did not seem to do the old man good. At least he nodded a few times powerfully, but then he fumbled in his breast-pocket for the old ragged notebook, wet his finger, opened to a specific page, and held it out to the child.

"Now read", he emitted contentedly, "read what sort of business I have concluded this evening with Chris Husen. Dear — very dear — but what should one do?"

And as the redhead now stared at the writing with avid eyes, there it stood recorded in large awkward letters, "To Chris Husen, 100 taler for little Fik".

"Yes", old Muhs continued, shaking his head, "they did not want to let it be cheaper. And for that I have bought you."

"Bought?", little Fik cried, her mind turning in circles for a moment.

And what now followed, it all slid and raged past like a mad, indescribable celebration. With glowing cheeks and sparkling eyes, as if an inner fever were shaking her, the redhead threw herself down before the old man, embraced his knees, kissed his feet, only to spring up again so that she could stroke his hard, bearded cheeks stormily with her soft child's hands.

"Now you have bought me, old Muhs", she cried ever anew.

And the Captain lowered his head thoughtfully, grumbling, "I have. But you are very expensive, girl. And now dance!"

Then this wild, strange festiveness again raged through the half-dark room.

***

Only, the more the Winter moved on, and the stronger the time of Christmas pressed, the more mono-syllabic and incommunicative the old bat began to become. With shock, the redhead perceived that her friend did not once show a sufficient interest in her dance arts anymore. For hours, the man would crouch in his chair again, and when he stared before himself so lost in thought, it not uncommonly occurred that a loud and tormenting groan forced its way out of his massive, labouring chest. More frequently, and for longer and longer, he placed himself before the black board, and seemed to whisper the three names to himself in endless repetition.

"Well just wait", little Fik thought, "I have something though which will bring you, you grumbly old fellow, onto other thoughts. Just look out!"

From the groschens which she had gradually saved from her housekeeping money, little Fik had in fact bought in the town a little music box. Fine, fine! It must be a splendid Christmas present for the Captain! For the girl had intuited finally with a sure instinct that this was a weakness of her protector, that even his darkest hours tended to be relieved by cheerful and pleasant music.

"Yes, yes", little Fik recalled from her studies at the village school, "the little Jew David had also brought old miserable Saul onto other thoughts this way. And what such an old musty man from the Bible can do, I have understood for a long time already."

And she kept a firm and defiant belief in that.

Outside on the streets and in the water meadows, the snow was falling more and more heavily, towering up walls, and building them soundlessly and closely around the quiet house. As a result, almost every noise which had previously penetrated to the two solitary people from the surrounding world died away. And it again became as dreary and silent as at the beginning of their acquaintance. And little Fik waited more and more anxiously and expectantly for the redemptive festivity. For she thought quite certainly that on this day something peculiar must occur. Truly, her expectation did not deceive her.

The morning of Christmas Eve broke. Then the first wondrous thing happened.

There were a few hard knocks on the front door, and before little Fik could spring out, she heard to her boundless astonishment how old Muhs rumbled down the steps, opened the heavy door, and finally received something.

What could it be?

She blinked breathlessly through a keyhole, and now she saw what the old man held in his hands. It was three massive wreaths, woven from dark leaves of laurel, which, bowed and stooped like never before, he shoved over his arm to climb up the steps again with his load, sombre and brooding to himself.

So that was it! Now the girl knew that it was today that the terrible, long-guessed event was impending for her. The mariner's memorial day had arrived, that fateful day on which the old man's most loved people in the world had drowned near the tip of Sumatra.

Without her really comprehending it, a tormenting distaste began creeping up on the redhead. Why did the old bat still trouble himself so senselessly and incomprehensibly? Had the fresh, life-loving creature next to him not made all her efforts to lighten the dark abyss in which he was foundering? Had she not attempted to conjure for him sun and moonlight in the midst of his night? And now everything shall have been in vain? She could not bear these thoughts.

"Wait", she thought, "you old, bristly, stupid rogue you, you shall have your cheerful Christmas Eve today though, whether you want it or not."

With this intent, she scurried busily back and forth, and when the afternoon had sunk down drearily and mistily over the earth, and the house already lay in night and darkness, she secretly planted three candles on the table in the secluded room, and before them she placed the precious music box. "Now come please", she wished defiantly. "But first I want to see what you do with your three wreaths, for you surely don't believe yourself, old Muhs, that I am leaving you alone with such heathen rubbish."

***

It thunders and crashes by the sea. The snowstorm whirls unrelentingly over the black surface, and when the white pieces of ice are tossed against each other by the fury of the water, then it is as if wild, whinnying voices are screaming and quarreling under the burst mantle.

"Hunger — hunger —", thus it then roars below. "We want to be full — want to devour the land and again be lords on earth like that time — that time before He came and spoke those words! The incomprehensible before which we must hide ourselves away! But now we want to be full — full!"

And then the easterly stamps with both feet on the still spreading ice crust until a new rift bursts open, and invisible sea gulls squawk and wail in delight in the air.

But do you also see the mole in the black mass, which stretches out like an uncanny, giant's arm into the sea — do you see there by the small lighthouse, whose light the raging easterly has long been booing — do you see the man in his hulking fur, how he stands there in order to toss wreath after wreath into the sea with shrill laughter?

Listen, and now the man is calling out, "I want to have my dead again, give them to me, for you owe me them! What? You don't want to? Then tell me at least the reason! I want to know the reason, for their time had not run out, and they did nothing to you. Each year I ask you about it, but I know that you pretend not to hear because you know nothing, because everything happens pointlessly, and that I don't want to endure!"

And now? What drives the man now? Is it possible? He stoops down, so low that he must plunge down any moment from the wet stones, and spits with mad fury into the thundering element.

"Shame on you — shame on you, it is all without sense and understanding. And I laugh at it!"

And now, do you hear? Do you hear his uncanny, shrill laughter? The sea gulls in the air scatter tumbling away from this sound, it rings out from the wall again, yes, even the spraying water listens for a moment and draws back from the wall.

But then another voice speaks, "Come, old Muhs, it's Christmas Eve!"

"What?"

"Dear, old old Muhs, it is Christmas Eve. And I have a present for you."

But straight afterwards, you no longer hear anything. For the water listens only for a moment to human fate, now it surges again and wants to draw everything which lives down from its heights.

"Higher", it sounds from below, "higher, so that we can fetch the both of them, the man and the child. They shall dance with us, they shall turn with us until all eternity. They shall celebrate our feast with us."

But from the beach it thunders back in answer as a never silenced call to battle, "Hunger — hunger."

***

They did not stride home together. The man walked ahead for a bit of the way, enveloped deep in his fur, and grumbling to himself turbid furious words which fell from his lips crumbling and disjointed, "What does the child want? What does the worm desire from me? I don't know her — I don't want her — I want to be alone like before, alone with my black board, and with the three crosses on it."

But these words, supplied by despair, were caught by the storming wind, and thrown here and there with mocking laughter, "Fly away, rabble!"

But behind the disturbed man, the child trotted. Her skirts rustled in the roaring easterly, yes, the storm had even whirled up her red hair, and now unfolded it like a red flag unrolling. No star illuminated the sky, but the flashing brilliance from little Fik's head spread a sort of shimmering light.

And if the storm had not howled with such a dull fury, and if the snowflakes had not pelted down so sharply and cutting, then you would certainly also have perceived the heavy sobbing of the redhead. Yes, she shook with fury and pity. And the supple body which she had not appropriately preserved against the cold, was incessantly shaken by a shivering and shaking until her teeth flew against one another as though with a chill.

"Now he will chase me away", she whispered, "today even, on Christmas Eve, for the dead are more dear to him than I am. And from now on, the old grumpy fellow will remain alone with them again. Oh, and at the same time, I had such a beautiful gift for him, and so dear!"

When she first seized on this thought, she started, and at the same moment, the girl was no longer capable of trotting like a dog behind the old man. With hostile ferocity rather, she struck her little fist against the storming flakes, but then she pulled herself together to whirl past the Captain with great flying leaps so that she could reach the empty house for certain before old Muhs.

Quite certainly. The surprise which she had planned, yes, the old grouch shall at least experience that. Later he would perhaps grieve when he found his little guest whom he had wanted to abandon today no longer in the solitary, wondrous house.

"Eh, and the hundred taler which he paid for me, he will lose that then too! Really, that would be good for him!"

Amidst these thoughts, she had reached the bat's home, and now she stormed up the dark steps as if hounded and chased.

***

"For all the world, what is that? What does that mean?", the man stammered quarter of an hour later in his snow-covered ragged fur, as he was rooted in rigid shock in the wide-open doorway which led to his living room.

There — there — for the sake of all mercy, what is it then? With his massive fists, he grasps at both door-posts to hold himself steady. Then he tilts his head, shoves his neck forward, and the grey protruding eyes under the white bushy brows are no longer able to construe the never-seen-before, wonderfully charming picture. How so much light shimmers towards him there! One — two — three. Yes, three thick, large candles are there, planted in heaps of sand on the table, and they are now flickering back and forth amiably. Wondrous shadows waver through the space, and the large room, lit up for the first time in a long time, looks like a solemnly serious hall in which the most beautiful festivity of humanity shall be had.

And now even these sounds! No, that is not possible. The old man has never heard the like. It streamed and rung out to him as it were, as if the most charming notes were pouring forth from quite tiny bells, straying in confusion, and intertwining into the most wondrous melody.

No, no, this time a dream must be ensnaring him. A gloriously shimmering conceit like had never penetrated this clouded disposition before. And the power of the notes floods into him so overpoweringly that the strong man must hold his heart with a sudden grip, because he thinks something in there would spring out, and he must now burst out in tears from pain or from joy over this wound. Yes, yes, in proper tears, so it is. Lightning quick, he lets one more glance sweep through the great empty space. But he finds himself alone, for the torn-up man does not notice that little Fik is cowering behind the hulking armchair to observe his actions with bated breath.

Who has done this, who has brought this wondrous instrument into his house? Oh, that is beautiful, that is wonderfully bright and good. And suddenly the overwhelmed man must creep to the table. There he taps about on the box with awkward finger, then he begins winding the handle anew, and as a cheerful melody climbs up to him now jingling and tinkling — he does not realise that he is hearing Gounod's Faust waltz — the storm tide of his reluctant emotions wrenches him to something outrageous. With his right hand, he must wipe away the streaming tears, but at the same time, something compels him to lift the powerful leg in the hulking waterproof boot.

God, God, he is alone, and he would not want it any other way. The giant claps his hands loudly, and then he begins slowly and solemnly to stride about the table. But soon it has become a rocking.

He is dancing!

God knows, the lonely, solitary man is really dancing. And at the same time, it tinkles and purrs from the box, and all the wavering shadows draw around him in friendly circles, yes, even the three candles on the black board leap one after the other, and begin the same impossible round dance as the old bat. Everything skips and springs in the wide room, and then the old man is not alone anymore either, but uncounted good thoughts and realisations dwell with him.

But now little Fik is also incapable anymore of restraining herself. Laughing and sobbing at the same time, she springs up, and claps her hands with joy over the dancing man.

"Old Muhs", she cries enraptured. "Old Muhs, now it'll be alright with you. And look out, the Christ child has brought you to your senses."

Then the old Captain stands stiff and still.

Only for a moment. For straight afterwards, he strides to the trembling thing, lifts her with a wild motion onto his arm, and as the box calmly plays on, the bat continues his solemn dance about the table with his load which he barely seems to notice.

"Little thing", he says clearly and distinctly to himself at the same time. "He can more than just bake bread.

Do you not see then that dear God stands back there on the board, having come again to me after so many years? And you yourself, little Fik, you must surely be a bit of a grandchild of his. Don't say anything, I knew that straightaway when I gave out the hundred taler for you. And because you are so excellent, I came out right cheaply by it."

Then the box was wound up anew, and the redhead slung both arms around the man's neck. And the solemn Christmas dance of this wondrous couple persisted until the three candles on the table had burnt down.

But in their hearts it gleamed brightly. As brightly as it can only gleam in the souls of the redeemed.

***

But I myself experienced the conclusion of this story. For, as a little boy, I knew the Captain and his wife. And this wife was called little Fik. On the evenings before Christmas, I often stood with other boys before the illuminated windows of the bat's home, and then one of us said to the others as we prodded each other in the side mysteriously, "You, pay attention, old Muhs up there is dancing again with little Fik. And they do that every Christmas."

Yes, yes, people must possess a music box for it. An artificial one, and also one in the heart. Otherwise such wondrous occurrences will never ever happen to them.

About the Publisher

Our mission is to provide translations into English of the complete works of neglected major European writers. We do not cherry-pick works that seem the most marketable, but rather seek to provide a complete collection of each writer's works so that readers can follow the writer's development and decide on its merits for themselves.

http://www.facebook.com/KANitzPublishing

http://www.kanitzpublishing.com